Lewis Mann is a qualified mechanical engineer and has spent many years in works engineering management and in engineering service management. Now retired, his many hobbies and interests include reading, painting, walking, music, as well as DIY crafts and has now decided to add writing to the list. He has been bandmaster of his local Salvation Army band for more than 45 years and has been married to his wife Joan for more than 50 years. He has three children and six grandchildren.

Lewis Mann

AFFA

AUSTIN MACAULEY PUBLISHERS™
LONDON * CAMBRIDGE * NEW YORK * SHARJAH

A CIP catalogue record for this title is available from the British Library.

ISBN 9781398424005 (Paperback)
ISBN 9781398424012 (ePub e-book)

www.austinmacauley.com

First Published (2021)
Austin Macauley Publishers Ltd
25 Canada Square
Canary Wharf
London
E14 5LQ

Prologue

Think of this… German soldiers during World War II; soldiers of the Third German Empire—the Third Reich—elite troops; the most efficient, disciplined and effective fighting force in the world at the time. Their weaponry was at the cutting edge of technology; even their uniforms were stylish as well as functional. They were a ruthless and efficient fighting force, and they had achieved their leader's ambition to conquer Europe and beyond. They were merciless in their subjugation of the countries they conquered as well as with the resistance groups which sprang up in many of these countries.

Now, think of the soldiers of the Roman Empire in the time of Christ. These soldiers were directly comparable to the soldiers of the Third Reich. They too were the most efficient, disciplined and effective fighting force in the world at that time. Their weaponry too was at the cutting edge of technology, and their uniforms too were equally as functional and stylish in their own time as those of the Third Reich. They had also achieved their leader's world conquering ambitions and were also ruthless in their subjugation of occupied countries and of the resistance groups within them.

When we watch films showing Roman Soldiers from Biblical times, we tend to think of them as dressed in armour-plated skirts with cumbersome headgear, brandishing spears or swords, forgetting that in their day, they were the most formidable fighting force in the world—a force which struck fear into the hearts of everyone with whom they came into contact.

This is the story of a small group of these men, a group that would have been under the command of an NCO such as a modern-day Sergeant. It tells of the problems they encountered in Judea around 33 AD, and how they dealt with them. They speak like soldiers do today. They act like soldiers do today. Imagine yourself in Judea at that time. Imagine you have just completed your basic training. Imagine you have been posted to Judea…

Chapter 1

It was one of the happiest times of my life. I had just passed out of the most prestigious military training school in a country whose Empire had spread across most of the known world. I had achieved my greatest ambition. I was what I had always wanted to be—an infantryman in the Imperial Roman Army. And now, I was travelling to my first posting.

I have to admit, it was not the best posting in the world. In fact, many newly qualified soldiers wouldn't have relished being sent here, to a place considered to be a nondescript backwater of the Roman Empire; hot, dirty, uncivilised in the main, and with a fractious and difficult populace. But to me, this posting was a challenge. I felt that if I could handle this, it would stand me in good stead in my army career. It would require soldiering of the highest quality and would look good on my record. Like everyone else, I was eager to start to climb the ladder of promotion and I had no doubt at all that this posting would help in no small way.

From my pre-posting briefing, I had learned that Judea had the dubious reputation of being one of the most difficult areas to administer of all the countries occupied by the Roman Empire at the height of its majesty and power. The Procurator, Rome's Military Commander in charge of Judea, was Pontius

Pilate—a cultured, introverted, self-taught expert in Judaism in his mid-forties. He was a career soldier who ruled with an iron hand over an indigenous population who were deeply rooted in their religious customs and practices. To preserve order, Pilate used diplomacy, tact and tolerance as well as brute force when necessary to manage these customs and practices, so that they did not interfere with Roman rules and principles and the furtherance of his career.

In addition to the official Judean hierarchy, Procurator Pilate faced a further serious problem: a number of Jewish Resistance movements, one of which was a fierce, well-armed and ruthless movement called the Zealots. This was a paramilitary group made up of well-established guerrilla fighters who knew their country inside out, and were willing and prepared to give their lives to establish its freedom from Roman occupation.

Nonetheless, I was happy to be travelling to Judea, to start my career in the Infantry of the Imperial Roman Army.

There were about twenty of us in the carriage, mostly seasoned soldiers, some coming back from leave, some being transferred to Judea and five of us newly qualified.

Dust rose from the wheels of the Troop Transport Carriage as we trundled on towards Jerusalem. The carriage, by civilian standards, was very well-appointed, comfortable and well sprung against the rigors of the poor roads we were travelling along. It was of a standard Roman military design, but because of the climate, doors had been removed and ventilation ports had been installed, meaning that we could taste the dry desert dust as it swirled up from the roadway.

The landscape had changed from pleasant and lush greenery at the point of our disembarkation in Judea to dry and arid desert as we made our way inland. Fields of wheat and barley interspersed with vines, fig trees and pomegranates as well as oranges and other citrus fruits dominated the coastal plain. I was surprised to see tulips, irises, cyclamen and daisies growing wild in the early part of our journey through Judea, but this landscape of plants and flowers changed abruptly as the geology changed. As the fertile plain started to be taken over by desert, rockrose and thorny broom turned the hillsides pink, white and yellow; all too soon, though, the desert properly started to take hold. The attractive fauna started to give way to prickly sabra cactus which only managed to exist by sucking moisture from deep beneath the desert sand. The desert was barren and foreboding; in its almost unbearable heat, nothing but these occasional spiky plants seemed to exist. We travelled on through a landscape which now was barren, the heat haze rising from the open ground and making the whole area appear to shimmer.

Our stopovers were at small military way stations around which small townships had grown up. But again, there was little to do; we merely stopped for overnight rest, refreshment and a change of coaching horses.

The rough craggy asperous environment was not only uninviting and brutal, but it also began to be boring—we seemed to be travelling through an endless cauldron of heat, grit and sand. And I was glad when eventually the landscape once again began to soften.

Now, we were entering a fertile valley and the sand, dust and rocky terrain was giving way to areas of grass and trees; yellow, harsh and burned at first, then becoming greener again as we approached Jerusalem.

For hours, we had been able to see the city walls in the distance. The nearer we got, the more we could hear the noise and clamour of a busy locality, and I soon realised that this was not some small backwater township but a vast imposing city bustling with life. We entered the city through a wide gateway in the city wall guarded by smart well-turned-out Roman troops, and then wound our way through the noisy and often narrow crowded streets. I began to realise how impressive the city was. I tried to remember what I had been told about the city in my pre-posting briefing, but nothing I recalled could have properly prepared me for what I saw. I began to become over-awed at the magnificent architecture and especially by the sheer size of the city. We travelled on through the clamorous colourful streets where stalls were piled high with fabrics, food, drink, spices, earthenware, pots and pans, even caged birds and animals; almost anything anyone could want. I was born and raised in a small Italian town, had even joined the army and done all my basic training in a town not much bigger, and had never even been to Rome or indeed, to any large bustling city like this before. And I greatly enjoyed taking in the smells, the atmosphere, the sights and the sounds of what seemed to me to be a vast metropolis.

Eventually, we turned into a broad street where Roman sentries stood at each side of a wide colonnaded archway. We stopped just inside the gateway where another two soldiers were checking people in. The carriage driver spoke briefly to one of them, who then checked a list and then waved us in to the headquarters of the Roman Occupation Forces in Judea.

*****

The barracks was, as I expected, a busy place. It had a paved area in front of the quite extensive administration offices and had neatly raked sand over a hard standing on the parade ground. A squad of men were drilling at one end, and other soldiers were running around the periphery of the parade ground in separate groups, while NCOs shouted disparaging remarks to encourage the men straggling at the back of each group to move faster. Our carriage finally came to a halt, and we collected together our kit and climbed down onto the hard standing in front of the offices.

Most of the guys dispersed in different directions to re-join their units, but the five of us who were new to the barracks were directed into a large room inside the administration block where an officer sat behind an imposing desk. A small aggressive NCO barked at us and brought us to attention. He walked sullenly down the line, picking at inconsequential breaches of uniform discipline. Then he stood to one side to allow the Officer to take over. We were given information about our new units and where to find our individual barrack rooms. Then we were dismissed and left to find our own way to our new homes. I had been told that my unit was commanded by Centurion Kaeso Cerius Isauricus. And my contubernium, the subdivision of ten men within my centurion's unit of one hundred men was led by an NCO—a Decanis, called Gaius Athamus. Of the five new starts, I was the only one in Decanis Athamus's unit, and after a couple of false starts, I managed to find my new home—my barrack room.

When I entered the barrack room, men were busy cleaning their kits, tidying their beds and lockers, and no one seemed, at first, to notice me. One of the guys was sitting on his bed, cleaning his dress uniform leather belt, and after a few moments, he glanced over in my direction.

"Hi. You must be the new guy," he said.

"Yes," I said, walking over to him and holding out my hand.

"I'm Tertius Mallius," I said, "Most people call me Tersh."

"Luce Macrinus—it's Lucius, really," he responded as he took my hand in a firm strong handshake.

"This is Tadius Justus. We call him TJ," said Luce, introducing me to the guy who was sitting on the next bed.

Luce had hardly got the words out of his mouth when a dark-haired shortish chubby man with broad sloping shoulders and the insignia of a Decanis on his uniform entered the room. Ignoring me now, Luce stood up and spoke to the man.

"Boss," he said, "we got a problem."

"What's up, lad?" asked the Decanis.

"Agatopus has been in. He's been through everybody's lockers looking for contraband."

"He'd better not have been through mine," said the Decanis, his face darkening in anger.

"No, no, he could go through ours because we are all minions, but apparently he's not allowed to go through yours unless you are present."

"Exactly," said the Decanis, wagging his finger to emphasise the point.

"But," continued Luce, "there's still a problem—look."

Luce pointed towards the top end of the room where the Decanis had his bed and locker. There, his locker was festooned with hemp twine secured in position with wax seals into which were pressed the insignia peculiar to the Military Police.

"They'll be back soon, you can depend on that," said Luce.

The Decanis suddenly started to bark orders to his men.

"Right," he said, "get the Syrians and tell them to bring their bag of tricks. I specially want a couple of scrapers, a candle and lighting materials—and some water. And tell them I want them NOW! The rest of you—spread out and keep a lookout for Agatopus and his cronies."

As he inspected the seals, I went and stood beside TJ who was watching the doorway. I asked him what the problem was but before he had a chance to answer, the Syrians—two non-combatant members of our contubernium (our unit of ten men) who were responsible for tasks such as general labouring, cleaning and maintenance work arrived with a hessian bag of tools each. One of them had the scrapers in his hand and handed them to the Decanis, then started to make a flame to light a stub of candle which he fished out of his hessian tool bag. The other started to pour water from a wineskin into an earthenware cup. Both Luce and the Decanis immediately set to work on the locker. The Decanis put the edge of the scraper up against one of the wax seals whilst Luce put the flame of the lighted candle near the base of the seal. The warmth of the candle flame quickly melted the base of the seal whilst the scraper prevented the polished wood of the locker from being burnt or marked with soot. He gently eased the seal off the locker, but as he did so, the insignia became completely disfigured. However, the Decanis didn't seem to be unduly worried, and started to work on another wax seal. Both he and Luce managed to quickly remove three seals and the hemp twine with them. They had planned which ones they needed to remove in order to be able to open one of the two locker doors.

"We're in!" said Luce as he opened the door. The Decanis reached inside and took out two hessian sacks, not unlike the tool bags which the Syrians had brought with them, except that each bag was tied around the top with hemp twine. He quickly passed the bags to TJ and said with urgency in his voice, "Get them to Jules straight away. And don't stop for anyone—especially Agatopus!"

TJ took the bags and left the barrack room quickly while the Decanis reached back inside the locker. He brought out a leather pouch. Rummaging in it, he pulled out a tiny block of beeswax and a small metal object with a wooden handle. He dropped the leather pouch to the floor then rubbed the metal part of the object in the beeswax. He left its end embedded into the beeswax and shut the locker door, then held one of the seals while Luce ran the candle flame on its underside and then positioned it in exactly the same place that it had been before they removed it. It still had the twine embedded into it but the insignia was now unrecognisable. Before it hardened, however, the Decanis picked up the small metal object with the wooden handle and pressed the metal part into the centre of the soft wax seal. The seal was perfectly restored because the small metal object with its polished wooden handle turned out to be a brand-new Military Police seal.

The two men quickly set to work on the other seals and soon the locker looked exactly as it did when I first saw it. The Decanis gently poured the water from the earthenware cup onto the seals in order to cool them, and then wiped them dry with care and dexterity which his manner and brusqueness had previously belied. Luce took the leather pouch and other tools which had been used.

"To Jules?" he asked.

The Decanis briefly nodded and Luce left the barrack room with the leather pouch stuffed down the front of his shirt.

"Right lads, back to work!" said the Decanis. He turned to me.

"Now lad," he said in a gruff and business-like manner, his accent betraying the fact that he had been brought up in a working-class area of Italy.

"I don't know what these blokes have told you about me but take note o' this—the best way me and you is goin' to get along is for you," and now he held out a short chubby forefinger, "to keep your nose clean," another pointing finger, "do as you're told," another, "and don't get in my way. Do them three things and we might be able to make something of you. You can call me Decanis, Dec, or Boss, I don't care, but not Sir. You'll end up calling me Affa like the rest of 'em do behind my back, I suppose. But I don't care as long as you behave yourself and do as you're told. Looks like you've already met the lads in my squad. You take this bed next to TJ's." He turned towards the rest of our group.

"Right lads, we're back to full strength for a change," he said with a satisfied grin then walked back towards his own bed at the far end of the barrack room.

As I started to unload my kit into my lockers, TJ walked back into the room and wandered over to me. We chatted briefly and in course of conversation, I asked him what all the commotion had been about and what had been in the hessian sacks. With a rueful smile and a shake of his head, he said, "Don't ask—best not to get involved, mate."

I never did find out what the panic had been about...but the saga didn't end there.

Later that same afternoon, we arrived back from a five-mile run complete with half pack, dumped our kits, and flopped down on our beds to recover. Almost immediately, however, Affa brought us to attention with a shout as an Officer accompanied by four soldiers walked into our barrack room. The officer was a tall lean man with receding fair hair. He had a livid scar on the left side of his face which went from the point of his jaw up to the side of his left eye. And he, along with the men with him, all wore the insignia of the Military Police. Immediately, they walked over to Affa who himself was also at attention.

"Athamus!" said the Officer in a menacing and overbearing manner, his hands clasped behind his back.

"Yes Sir!" said Affa, almost shouting his reply.

"Your locker?"

"Yes Sir!"

"Everybody's lockers are being searched," the Officer said abruptly. With a wave of his hand but no further explanation as to why the search was being carried out, he indicated to his men to open Affa's locker. The seals were removed with none of the care that Affa had displayed, so much so that Affa, aware that he outranked the soldiers who were opening the locker said, "Be careful lads, I look after that locker!"

"Quiet!" shouted the Officer and took a step nearer to Affa so that he was now eyeballing him, his nose only a couple of inches from Affa's cheek. Affa didn't reply but neither did he move his head. He looked straight ahead, appearing not to be intimidated in any way by the Officer.

"Nothing here, Sir," said one of the soldiers who had searched Affa's locker.

The Officer didn't speak, neither did he move. For a long moment, Affa and the Officer stayed at this impasse. Then the officer turned and walked towards the locker. Slowly and deliberately, he pulled out a number of items, all personal—papyrus rolls, letters, trinkets, keepsakes, cleaning materials, belts and boots, all of which he threw behind him onto the floor. Then, his hands once more clasped behind his back, he turned and walked back to Affa. Without speaking, he eyeballed him once more, then turned and walked down the barrack room, roughly kicking the kit which had been left on the floor and throwing it off the beds and on to the floor. Once more, he turned and, hands again clasped behind him, casually walked back towards Affa. Kicking his way through some of Affa's personal belongings which he himself had thrown on the floor, he faced Affa nose to nose and shouted at the top of his voice.

"Get this place tidied up, it's a pigsty!!!"

He turned to the rest of us and continued his tirade,

"That goes for the rest of you too! You'll all find yourselves on a charge if I catch this room in this state again!"

He turned and slowly walked towards the door but he stopped at the bed nearest to the door where one of the lads, whom I found out later to be called Cass, was standing at attention.

"And you! Get your hair cut! You're a disgrace to your uniform!"

He left the barrack room accompanied by his men. Affa waited until they were well out of earshot then brought us at ease and then to dismissal.

He smiled a wry smile, “Get this pigsty cleaned up, you lot, we don’t want the PIGS to move in with us, do we?” he said.

Chapter 2

Over the next few weeks, I got to know the lads well; they seemed a decent bunch, though from a very varied selection of backgrounds. Luce, perhaps because I had met him first, took me under his wing, showed me the ropes so to speak, and we soon became firm friends.

Affa himself seemed to me to be a bit of a paradox; he enforced Army rules and regulations whilst at the same time, shamelessly bending the rules to suit himself. Luce's appraisal of him was straightforward. "Not a bad boss," he said, "a few rough edges—well, all the edges are rough, actually! But he does look after us and he's a good soldier. And because he speaks Hebrew pretty well, he can get civilian stuff we might need at a good price. Mind you, he looks after himself as well, but he always seems to be able to get us what we need by fair means or foul—mainly foul I think! Put it this way: I'm glad he's on our side and not theirs!"

Affa had a way of speaking which was typical of the area where he had been born and brought up. His name, Gaius Athamus, meant 'rich harvest' which didn't suit him one bit. 'rough diamond' would have been a more suitable description. But he pronounced his name 'Affamus', the shortened version of which provided the lads with the perfect nickname for him. Thanks to his way of speaking, Affa he had become, and Affa he remained all the time I knew him.

Affa's contubernium (the squad of ten men he was responsible for) consisted of himself plus seven soldiers and two Syrian labourers. The two Syrians were not fighting men, they were simply responsible to Affa for the cleanliness of the Squad room, and they also carried out all the other menial labouring tasks. These men, however, were far more than labourers. They were craftsmen too. And as well as labouring, they undertook the work of carpentry, repairing barrack room fittings and furniture, blacksmithing and farrier work with respect to the handling of the mule which our contubernium was responsible for.

Of the fighting men in our contubernium, besides Luce and TJ, there was Decius Gallus—a tall intelligent athletic soldier with a very enquiring mind, very interested in technology. As we all had shortened names or nicknames for each other, Decius was known as Dess. He could explain exactly how any of the weaponry and equipment we used worked, and if any piece of kit got broken and the Syrians weren't able to repair it, we knew Dess would find a way of fixing it.

At the other end of the 'technology spectrum' was Justus Calvinus or 'Cal' as we called him. Cal was a pleasant enough guy who was completely baffled by anything technical, and who was, in addition, the most accident-prone person I have ever met. Even the tools and weapons we used regularly were a mystery to him. As long as they worked as they should, Cal was happy with them. Once anything went wrong, however, he was totally lost. His usual solution to that type of problem was to ask Dess for help.

Cassius Sentius was a very quiet, pensive and serious-thinking man. Although he was easy to get on with—they all were—Cass was a deep thinker and seemed unable ever to brush things off lightly. Most soldiers can simply follow orders even if they don't understand or agree with them. Cass found it difficult to do that. He was a good soldier and always followed orders and did as he was told, but he did tend to brood over things he didn't agree with or understand.

Every outfit has its comedian, and ours was no exception. Cato Sidonius was a real wit. He seemed to be able to find a witty and amusing one-liner for any occasion, however fraught, however serious. A good and reliable soldier, Cato had been well educated and could use his sharp and often incisive wit to make a point or to combat the stupidity of bureaucracy. This didn't always go down well with his superiors, though. And it got him into trouble on more than one occasion. He was also a little on the chubby side—chubby enough, in fact, for him to be nicknamed 'Porky'!

I soon settled into a regular soldier's lifestyle, and enjoyed every minute. My first few weeks consisted of a continual round of kit inspections, exercises, physical training, weapons training, marksmanship, forced marches and cross country runs, as well as guard duties both in barracks and in the city, and day and night patrols. Affa always pushed us hard in order to keep us at the peak of fitness and efficiency, and I soon realised that when we were out on ops, we would be a force to reckon with. Surprisingly enough though, my first proper operation in my new unit didn't involve fighting efficiency, it revolved around a quality that I didn't even realise Affa possessed, that of diplomacy!

Our unit had been detailed to oversee the apprehension and arrest of an itinerant preacher and Baptist who was causing trouble for the Hebrew King Herod. Our orders were to accompany Herod's Royal Guard to ensure there was no trouble because they did have a reputation of being rather bull-headed when trying to sort out even the simplest of problems. Our procurator, Pontius Pilate, held no brief for Herod. In fact, he treated him and his entourage with a large amount of contempt. Herod was merely a puppet dictator; a corrupt Tetrarch who ruled his people (the people of Galilee and Perea) in collusion with our occupation forces, more often than not using his power to further his own interests. Affa had, on this occasion, been given discretionary powers to intervene if necessary because it was felt that there may well be trouble.

Although our unit was an infantry unit not cavalry, our training as infantrymen had included horsemanship. We were taught how to ride and control our horses, but not taught in the art of fighting on horseback. As far as infantrymen were concerned, horses were a form of quick and convenient transportation. On this operation, we went on horseback to Herod's palace to meet up with a small mounted detachment of the Royal Guard and rode with them out of the city limits and on towards the Jordan river where we saw a large group of people on the shore and a smaller group wading in the water.

Out of courtesy, Affa held us back and let the Royal Guard go on a little way in front until we arrived at the shore. As we approached, a few of the groups on the shore looked at us with some obvious apprehension; some even turned and started to leave. The man in charge, however, a tall muscular man dressed in a rough shirt and standing up to his hips in water, virtually ignored us and carried on preaching and baptising the people around him as if we weren't there at all. There were three or four people with him, organising and helping, who were also trying not to be intimidated by our appearance on the shore.

Our unit, Affa at the head of us, stayed mounted on horseback watching, while the captain of the Royal Guard and the rest of his unit dismounted, and walked to the edge of the river. The Captain was a short arrogant man, and his second in command was much the same. The second in command had a coil of rope over his shoulder, and another Royal Guardsman had a set of heavy chains and manacles in his hands.

"You!" shouted the Captain towards the Baptist. He ignored the shout.

"You, Baptist—I am here to arrest you on behalf of King Herod!"

The Baptist finished what he was doing. Then, languidly, he turned to face the Captain.

"Are you speaking to me?" he asked with an attitude of obvious contempt.

"Yes. Come out of the water immediately, you are under arrest!"

The Baptist rolled his eyes skyward and turned back to the business of baptising his followers, completely ignoring the Captain of the Guard, amid a smattering of laughter from his followers.

The Captain, obviously annoyed and frustrated at having been humiliated in front of both his own men and the Baptist's followers, started shouting once more, and was now ordering his men to take the Baptist by force. The Baptist's men in the river moved closer to their leader, taking an aggressive stance. And a number of his supporters on the shore armed themselves with stones and started wading into the river to add their muscle to the confrontation which was developing. It was also clear to us that the Baptist himself was unwilling to go quietly, and we all felt that this was a potentially explosive situation which was going to get out of hand and result in a major clash. Luce already had his hand on the hilt of his sword, so I did the same, although Affa seemed to be more relaxed than any of us.

Affa decided to intervene. Still mounted, he calmly walked his horse to the side of the Captain of the Royal Guard and ordered him to be quiet.

"Give your reins to him," said Affa pointing to me as I was the soldier nearest to him at the time, "and move back." Looking at me, he said "You follow me and bring his horse." He turned to the other men in our unit and said, "The rest of you stay here."

Affa walked his horse into the river and, indicating to the Baptist's followers to move away, rode right up to the man who had now drawn himself up to his full six feet, six inches height, and had folded his muscular arms across his chest. He looked at Affa with a defiant expression and a half smile. Affa, still on horseback, had put himself between the Baptist and his followers, and now he leaned forward and spoke quietly and privately to the man.

"Look lad," he said in a calm and easy manner, "we can do this in one of two ways. We can either wait for five minutes and let you wind up your business here, then you can mount this horse and ride back to the city with my men in a dignified manner, or we can give you a good hiding and take you by force. Either way, you'll end up coming back to town with us. I know you're a big lad and can look after yourself, but there's eight big lads here who enjoy a good scrap, and you'll end up walking back to Jerusalem in chains, pulled along by my men, bruised, bloodied and humiliated. And there's no dignity in that!"

Affa sat up straight once more.

"It's up to you lad," he said, "Your call."

The Baptist had been silent all the time Affa had been speaking, but had held Affa's eye in a defiant faceoff. Without speaking, he continued to stare at Affa, obviously mulling over what had been said to him. Finally, after what seemed like an eternity, he turned towards his followers, unfolded his arms, and spread them out at his sides.

"Friends," he said, "I'm told that King Herod wants to speak to me. Perhaps, he wants to repent his sins!" he said with a smile, and again there was laughter from his followers.

"My disciples here will continue my work, and I will be back here with you all very soon. God bless you all!"

With that, the Baptist turned towards me and took the reins from my outstretched hand. He leapt up easily onto the horse, reined it round, and started to walk it towards the rest of our unit on the shore.

"Hey, what about me—that's my horse," shouted the Captain of the Royal Guard to Affa.

"I've requisitioned it," said Affa, with a look on his face which showed an equal amount of contempt to that which the Baptist had shown earlier.

"I suggest you hitch a ride from one of your lads."

Affa started to walk his horse after the Baptist. Then, almost as an afterthought, he turned and shouted over his shoulder, "Or walk," before turning back and following the rest of us as we made our way towards the Jerusalem road.

Luce was now riding beside Affa. "What was that all about, Boss," he asked, "What did you say to him?"

Affa smiled and tapped his nose, "If I told you, you would be as clever as me," he said.

"Well, it certainly did the trick," said Luce.

"It saved us a lot of hard work, lad. That's the main thing," said Affa.

All of the lads in our unit were suitably impressed at Affa's skills of diplomacy. Somehow, I hadn't seen him as any kind of diplomat, and had expected to sample his skills as a front-line soldier before I witnessed any sort of diplomacy skills. As yet though, I had only experienced exercises, physical training, routine patrols and so on. However, soon we were assigned to a special operation, and I was to sample Affa's skills as a soldier first hand.

Chapter 3

Much of our work involved policing the local populace, keeping order and ensuring that Roman law and order was being upheld and that the streets were safe not just for Romans but for everyone. We were also involved in shows of military strength to sap the will of the occupied peoples, and finally, to crush the resistance movements, mainly the strongest and best armed of these—the Zealots.

Named Zealots because of the zealous and fanatical way in which they fought against our occupying forces, they represented a principle and a policy that other Jewish groups did not share. The other groups who opposed the occupation of their country were the Sadducees, the Pharisees and the Essenes. The Sadducees seemed to live a good life, seeking power in high places, sometimes even collaborating with Roman authorities in order to achieve this. The Pharisees, on the other hand, believed that it was their God's will to live in the world in which he had placed them, yet to remain pure, and to meet and cope with the temptations, dangers and trials they faced in a heroic and stoic manner. The Essenes simply ran from confrontation and conflict, taking refuge in their isolated desert communes. The Zealots, then, were our major headache—they were a paramilitary group which was well organised with a clear line of command from a top-level Executive Unit right down to the 'soldiers' on the front line. Each small front-line fighting group was responsible to the Executive Unit, and each of these groups knew well the area in which it worked. The Zealots were prepared to confront opposition directly and head on, and were more than willing to fight fanatically and even to die for their cause.

My first encounter with the Zealots was a real 'trial by fire' and came only a few weeks after the Baptist incident.

By now, I had been in Affa's squad for quite a while when we were detailed to be part of the escort squad for a new consignment of goods which had been shipped in from Italy. On a fairly frequent basis, we would receive supplies of a variety of goods such as uniforms, ammunition, weaponry, administration supplies and even home comforts such as speciality Italian food direct from home. Even though our Quartermasters and Admin Orderlies made use of local suppliers, much of the stuff these people supplied was of a far inferior quality to Roman goods. So, these supplies, direct from 'Blighty,' were welcomed by us all and were a real boost to morale. From time to time, the resistance movements, and the Zealots in particular, had harassed supply convoys travelling between the coast and Jerusalem. It wasn't a big problem because they were afraid of direct confrontation, so the harassment normally only consisted of niggles like finding barricades across the roads, bridges damaged or torn down and so on. There had been one or two 'hit and run' attacks when bandits had attacked the convoys at places where the cover was suitable for them to do so. They would attack using slingshot, and sometimes with stolen crossbows, then they would use the cover of the landscape and their knowledge of the terrain to get away before we could engage them. On any occasion when this happened, our Engineer and Pioneer Corps would clear the areas concerned and ensure that any suitable cover was removed so that it couldn't happen again. So, bit by bit, we were making the roads safe not only for ourselves but for anyone who used them.

We had taken over the escort duty from a military outpost about twenty miles from Jerusalem, and although we were travelling over roads, we knew reasonably well there had been one or two skirmishes in that area over the previous month and there was a general feeling of unease amongst us.

That accounted for the tense nervous silence as the supply convoy and escort made its way steadily towards Jerusalem. The only sound was the noise of the horses' hooves, the squeak of leather and the grinding of the iron-bound carriage wheels on the dusty roadway. I caught a movement out of the corner of my eye over to my left. But when turning, all I saw was the harsh arid landscape shimmering in the heat of the day. Suddenly, there was a shout from the front of the convoy; the Decanis on front point had been hit by a missile and bandits were approaching, hurling missiles and brandishing swords, daggers, crossbows and spears. The lads told me later that they had never ever seen Zealots so well-armed. In seconds, the resistance fighters were swarming down from the front with their faces covered with cloths to preserve their anonymity. A second group came into view from my left, where I had just been looking and had seen nothing. It looked as if we might be outnumbered and the resistance fighters appeared to think so too, and were clearly emboldened by the fact. Still, we all expected that they would soon turn tail and run for the hills as they usually did, and we were taken by surprise when they continued to engage. We, escort troops, deployed to meet them head on, and soon, we were involved in hard bloody hand-to-hand fighting. As we fought, the carriage drivers tried to control the carriage horses which had been spooked by the noise and commotion going on around them. We definitely were outnumbered. However, we were better equipped, better trained and more disciplined than the bandits. And in a short time, we were able to overwhelm them. The fighting was hard and ruthless on both sides, and I was impressed by the way Affa directed and led us. We fought in a soldierly and disciplined fashion, and although a number of soldiers were badly injured and some even killed, none of our unit were injured. We seemed to have been skirmishing for an age, but I guess it was only a matter of around twenty to thirty minutes before we fought them off and some of the escort troops were giving chase to mop up the stragglers. We counted the cost. We tended to the wounded troops and rounded up the prisoners; some of them were still being belligerent. And I have to admit that some of our lads who were still fired up with the fight treated them with the contempt we all felt that they deserved.

As we were trying to restore some kind of order once more, two dispatch riders arrived from Jerusalem. They had been sent to warn us of possible bandit attacks because there had been a serious insurrection in Jerusalem, and rebels–thought to be Zealots—had attacked prominent administration buildings, and had murdered some Jewish leaders who they thought had been collaborating with the occupying forces. Jerusalem troops were engaging and trying to re-establish calm and order. All units outside the city were instructed to return with great caution and as much speed as possible to Jerusalem in order to reinforce the troops there. We guessed that because we had already engaged with bandits, they wouldn't be back in a hurry. So, we threw caution to the wind and made fast headway to Jerusalem. The city was in a state of chaos. It was in total lockdown; people had been told to stay off the streets and had been warned that anyone caught on the street would be summarily executed. Herds of cattle and sheep as well as oxcarts and other heavy equipment had been used to block the entrance roads to our barracks, and our unit was one of those deployed to herd the animals out of the way and remove the barricades and obstacles until the city was brought back to order again. Martial Law was tightened citywide for a month until the city was back to normal and most of the known Zealot leaders were rounded up and imprisoned. Two of them were still at large—not main men but still well up in the echelons of Zealot leadership. The more important of the two was Jesus Barabbass. This man was popular with the local people and we were told that he had been spirited away by them and hidden in a local safe house.

At the barracks, interrogation of the prisoners who had been caught during the insurrection had been ruthless, and it was soon established that Barabbass's likely hideout was a safe house in south Jerusalem. Plans were laid to apprehend him, and our unit was included in the battalion deployed to seek him out and bring him to justice.

We were one of four units detailed to capture him, although this time our unit was to be the reserve force just engaged as back up. We were all blacked for night ops and our weapons and equipment wrapped in cloths to prevent any noise as we moved. It was around two o'clock in the morning, but as it was a moonlit night, we could still see the rear of the safe house quite clearly in the distance. Our intelligence had determined that there would be dogs at the house and a number of bodyguards with Barabbass, but we had a good unit as the main assault party and were fairly certain that we wouldn't require to be deployed. A scout group had gone out earlier and dealt with the dogs, feeding them with drugged meat. All was quiet. We watched and waited. Suddenly, there was a commotion at the front of the house as the main attack group burst the door down and forced their way in. There was a lot of noise, shouting and women screaming. We saw men leaping out of the back windows of the house and a skirmish between them and our secondary assault group which was stationed behind the house. Soon, our lads had wrestled and fought them to the ground and the operation seemed to be coming to a satisfactory conclusion.

"That's the idea," said Affa, leaning back against a tree stump and starting to relax, "We can rest easy lads, nothing for us to do this time." He had hardly finished speaking when out of the darkness, two men stumbled into us. They seemed to be as surprised as we were but fortunately, we reacted more quickly than they did. And although they fought fanatically and struggled to get free, there was eight of us and only two of them, so we soon had them pinned to the ground, and Dess and Porky were securing their hands behind their backs with leather cuffs. Affa sent a runner to the main group to tell the Commander we had apprehended some prisoners. We were told to bring them to the safe house where informers had been brought in to identify exactly who had been caught and if Barabbass was with them.

The rest of us waited outside while Affa, Dess and Porky took the prisoners back into the safe house to be identified. A few minutes later, the lads came out followed by Affa with a beaming smile on his face.

"Listen," he said quietly to us all as he indicated that we should all gather around him, "We watched them run from the house, chased them down, and caught them, ok? That's the story."

"Ok Boss," said Luce, "Did they get Barabbass then?" he asked.

"No," said Affa with one of his sly grins, "WE did!!!"

Chapter 4

For the next couple of months, our duties revolved once more around exercises and physical training, lectures on new weaponry, administrative duties in barracks and daylight patrols in Jerusalem itself. These daylight patrols were a totally different type of work to the night operations we had been on—more related towards showing the power and might of Rome than anything else. Locals didn't usually step out of line when they saw us around the city, and because we always patrolled well-armed and in unit strength, we rarely encountered problems. I quite enjoyed these day patrols—it was a chance to look and feel like real soldiers resplendent in full dress uniform, to show the might and power of Rome, a chance to be on show. The youngsters would look at us in awe. The men would look at us with a respectful contempt. And the women seemed to like men in uniform.

Night patrols in the city, however, were a different matter. None of us relished them. Zealots would hide in the shadows, watching for an opportunity to kill occupation soldiers. Some of these Zealots were shepherds who were experts in the use of the slingshot, and would expertly take out soldiers at the back of a night patrol group and then simply melt back into the darkness. Noisier areas of the city were worse because slingshot snipers used the noise to cover the sound of the whirling of the slingshot before a lethal missile was let loose. Some units, I was told, had lost a number of men on night patrols, and we were advised never to take any chances.

Affa's advice to us was, as usual, straightforward, simple and to the point.

"Don't ever forget that they are always on the lookout for an opportunity to kill you! You've got be as ruthless as they are," he advised, "You don't give them a chance to get near you, and above all, you don't trust ANY of them!"

It was against rules and regulations to fraternise with the locals or to go into town alone at night. In fact, some areas of the city were strictly off limits to us at all times when we were off duty, even during the day because of the danger from Zealot assassins. We were told that even women and children were used by resistance fighters to lure unsuspecting soldiers to their deaths.

We knew, though, that some guys in our battalion still risked going into some of these areas but none of our contubernium ever did—or so we thought. So, when Affa came into the barrack room in a furious rage one morning, we were all shocked to find that one of our colleagues had formed a relationship with a civilian woman in the city during his time off duty, and had been murdered by Zealots. But to our surprise, we soon realised that Affa was more annoyed that one of his men had disregarded his advice than he was about the fact that the soldier had been murdered.

"Take note, you lot," he said gruffly to us all, "Calvinus has not only got himself killed, he's also put the rest of us at risk because of his stupidity and weakness!"

"At risk, Boss?" asked TJ, "Why are *we* at risk because of what *he's* done???"

"We're at risk because he's reduced our unit strength by one man again. And he's weak because he got himself killed by getting involved with a *woman*!"

"A woman?" said Dess with a look of amazement on his face. None of us were aware that Cal had been seeing anyone, and in addition, it seemed quite out of character.

"Yes," said Affa, his face red with rage, "A woman he knew nothing about, and who turned out to be working with the Zealots. She was even married to one, it turns out!"

"I've told you all before," he continued, turning and addressing all of us, finger wagging as usual, "Don't trust ANY of them. Keep 'em all at arm's length! Now I have to make a report out about the idiot. More unnecessary work he's caused me!"

Affa stormed out.

"All heart, isn't he?" said Luce to no-one in particular.

The loss of a man was indeed a blow to us. By that time, in the history of the Roman Empire, Centurions commanded only 80 fighting men, not a hundred as the name suggests. When the military hierarchy was originally set up, a hundred men was the standard unit size, and labouring staff were extra. But expansion of the Empire and the need to police it meant that more officers were required against the number of enlisted men. Subsequently, the Centurion became a leader of only eighty fighting men with a support group of twenty non-combatant labourers. This group was then sub-divided into ten smaller units each commanded by a Decanis, and each comprising eight combatant and two non-combatant men, often Syrian civilians. Affa's contubernium had been made back up to full strength by my arrival. Before I had arrived, one of his men had been killed in a skirmish with resistance fighters, and I had been sent to replace him. Now his unit was reduced once more to six fighting men, seven including himself.

We learnt that the temple guard, a Jewish paramilitary force maintained by the local Jewish Temple hierarchy to keep the peace between the local populace and especially to police the Temple area, had some intelligence about the woman who had been involved in our colleague's murder. Affa often spoke disparagingly about the Temple Guard—the 'Toy soldiers' as he called them. But it has to be said that they appeared to have a good and very efficient intelligence gathering department within their organisation. Our Military Police under Agatopus worked closely with them and followed up a number of leads to try to bring someone to justice for the death of Cal. For several weeks, on and off, they followed through on leads, arresting suspects and keeping others under surveillance. However, we were eventually told that it was thought that the woman and her associates had left Jerusalem soon after Cal's death and they were unable to bring anyone to justice for the crime. Agatopus had carried out reprisals, and some hostages had been taken from the local populace and executed. But no-one was ever charged with Justus Calvinus's murder. However, the incident did teach the rest of us an important lesson. Cal was the last soldier from our battalion ever to lose his life that way.

Chapter 5

Of all the duties we had to perform in Judea, the most distasteful to me was the carrying out of capital sentences imposed on felons and resistance fighters who had been found guilty of offences. I felt that we were soldiers, not executioners, but the local judiciary were not allowed to carry out capital punishment. So floggings and executions always had to be carried out by the occupation forces. The most heinous of executions was the crucifixion—a type of tortuous execution designed by Rome to inflict a painful and lingering death in the most humiliating and public way. The prisoner was literally nailed to a wooden scaffold through hands and feet so that he had to push down on his feet to take the weight off of his arms and ease the pain in his chest and of the nails through his hands, to enable him to breathe. Eventually, the prisoner becomes unable to do this and he dies of asphyxiation in unbearable agony. I had witnessed crucifixions, but always from a distance. And I certainly had never been a member of an execution squad. Affa, however, had taken part in a number of them and in fact, had been in charge of many of them, and knew the procedure well. He had quite an unforgiving attitude, and felt that since the prisoners had been tried and found guilty of their crimes, they must deserve the sentence they had been given. His way of dealing with the job was to remain detached completely from the victims as people. To him, they were just vermin which had to be disposed of, another job to be done, and done in a soldierly and efficient manner. All the rest of the lads had seen or been involved in so many that they too had mostly become desensitised, and were no longer able to show any compassion to the victims. TJ told me he had no feelings of compassion of any sort for the victims.

"To be honest," he said, "Luce, although he never baulked at any of the crucifixion or flogging duties, is the only guy I have ever seen showing any pity to victims, even though it might only be to say 'poor beggars' as they screamed in agony as the nails were hammered into their hands before rising up in the air on to the scaffold. I could tell he genuinely felt for them. But it never bothered me one bit."

So far, I had been fortunate. I hadn't had to witness or take part in any crucifixions at all. In fact, I had been in Affa's squad more than a year before we were assigned to officiate at a crucifixion.

A man had been arrested by the Jewish temple police for some religious charge or other. I wasn't sure at the time what it was all about, but I did know he had a big following among the common populace. He seemed to be at odds with much of the orthodox Jewish religious teaching, and in this he had fallen foul of the Jewish authorities. The occupation forces had got involved because his crime, the Jews said, warranted a capital sentence. The rumour we heard was that he was claiming to be the king of the Jews, which didn't make any sense to us. As far as we were concerned, Herod was their king.

He had been arrested and brought in from his hiding place on the Mount of Olives by the Temple Guard, so we knew very little about him. To say he was supposed to be a king, he looked very unremarkable, like a hundred other farm workers and fishermen in the countryside outside the city walls, in fact.

Our shift started much as normal; we checked on parade and had a kit inspection. As usual, Affa was satisfied if everything was there and in a reasonable condition. His main concern was always that our weapons were all in order and serviceable. As he often reminded us, the condition of our weapons could mean the difference between life and death not just for us, but for him also, and that to him was the most important factor! We were told that the patrol we had been originally scheduled to carry out had been assigned to another squad, and we were told to stand by ready to hold this prisoner in close custody. Apparently, he had become very important.

"This bloke seems to be the flavour of the month," said Cass.

As it happened, his fate was decided in much less than a month, but the repercussions would be worldwide and would last much longer. But of course, back then we had no idea of that.

We were beginning to think they weren't going to transfer him. He had been examined and interrogated by Pilate and also by Herod, the Judean King who was allowed to rule by Pilate as long as he kept the populace under tight control—a job he enjoyed doing and a job he did ruthlessly. The prisoner had even been offered a free pardon by Pilate as a token of goodwill in an effort to keep the Jews in good humour and avoid trouble. However, the crowd appeared not to want him freed, instead asking for Barabbass of all people. When we heard Barabbass was to be released, we could hardly believe it. Luce asked Affa about it.

"Do you honestly think Barabbass will get far?" Affa answered, "They might make it look as though they have freed him but I guarantee he will be dead by this time tomorrow!"

So, the prisoner was eventually handed over to us by the Temple guard. They had no jurisdiction as regards Capital Punishment, and he had now been condemned by Pilate not to be crucified but to be flogged instead. As we were duty squad, it was our responsibility to ensure the punishment was meted out. The prisoner was brought into our lockup by the Temple Guard and Affa sorted out the transfer details.

"Take good care of him," the Temple Guard officer said to him laughing, "He's the king of the Jews apparently!"

With a wry smile, Affa retorted, "Don't you worry, we know how to treat kings here! We'll give him the full 'king' works!"

He turned to us.

"Right," he said, pointing to the papyrus note he held, "it says here, he's to be flogged. Let's get on with it!"

He walked over to the wall and unhooked two of the many-thonged whips which were hanging there, each by a leather loop on the end of the handle.

"Here, lad," he said to me, "You and TJ can have the privilege. TJ will show you how it's done. Luce, you and Porky get our 'king' set up."

Luce and Porky roughly frogmarched the man to a nine-inch-diameter wooden post standing in the middle of the open yard. Using chains and ropes, they secured him to the post after stripping him naked. His back was now exposed ready for TJ and me to use the whips which we had been given by Affa. They were both multi-thonged whips with some of the thongs knotted at the ends and others with pieces of bone or sharp bits of metal attached to inflict even more pain to the victim as they tore at his flesh.

"Right lads," said Affa, "Let's see what you can do!"

TJ strode up to the flogging post. He had done this before and knew exactly what to do. He whipped the air a couple of times to limber up before bringing the whip back and with as much force as he could summon, administering a devastating blow to the man's naked back. The prisoner cried out in pain as the thin leather thongs bit into his skin and the bits of bone and metal ripped at his flesh. TJ took a step back and nodded to me, indicating I should do the same as he had just done. I have to admit, I didn't show any compassion to the man. I felt that this was just another part of my job. And I was young and ambitious, determined to make a name for myself and unwilling to show any weakness in front of my mates. Any task I was given, I had tried to carry out with enthusiasm and ardour, and this was no exception. Copying TJ, I limbered up and then I drew back the whip in the same way he had before bringing it back down with as much force as I could muster, administering a blow equally as vicious as TJ's had been. We took turns in this way, regardless of the cries and obvious suffering of the man who began to bleed profusely, and was obviously in great pain.

It soon became difficult for TJ and me to stand up and keep our balance—we were slipping around because of the blood on the floor at the base of the flogging post, and one of the Syrian labourers was summoned by Affa to throw down water and mop up the prisoner's blood. When they had mopped up, we looked over at Affa but he simply indicated that we carry on, so we continued with the flogging—first TJ, then me, then TJ again and so on.

I was beginning to think we were going to flog him to death but eventually, Affa stopped us.

"Alright, he's had enough," he said. A Syrian threw water in the prisoner's face to bring him round as he was almost unconscious by now, and Luce and Porky unchained him and half marched, half dragged him away from the flogging post. Still naked, he was shivering from the cold water and from shock. Luce took an old horse blanket from the corner of the room and threw it around the man's shoulders. His body and hands shaking, he painfully tried to pull it round himself and then turned to Luce, hoarsely thanking him.

"Hey, that's no good," Affa said, pointing at the drab grey-coloured horse blanket. "This bloke's a king—this is what we need!" He picked up a purple chintz cover that had once been an expensive table cover (plunder from an action we had taken part in a few days before in the City, and which Affa later sold to make some beer money for the lads). Purple had long been a regal colour in Italy, a colour associated with Kings, Queens and Emperors. Affa roughly pulled off the horse blanket, making the prisoner wince in pain once more, and then he carefully put the purple table cover round the prisoner's shoulders as if he were indeed helping to dress a man of great importance.

"That's more like it," he said. "Hey, I know what else we need," he added with a wry smile on his lips, "Where's those heavy leather gauntlets we have?"

"The Armourer's gloves? Out in the mess room," said Luce.

Smiling, Affa disappeared into the mess room, then reappeared pulling the heavy gloves onto his chubby hands. He went outside into the small kitchen garden behind the Guardroom.

"Here's what he needs," he shouted as he came back into the Guardroom, "a nice laurel wreath fit for a king!" In his hands, he held a long Nabk weed he had cut from the garden area. The weed was very prevalent in and around Jerusalem, and the Syrians often had to clear them from the kitchen garden. It had lush green leaves similar to ivy leaves. The stem of the weed was strong but pliant, and was thickly covered in sharp thorns, each at least an inch in length. Affa started to weave the stem into a circular coil very similar to a Roman Emperor's laurel wreath with the ends twisted against themselves to hold the coil together.

"Here we are," he said as he walked towards the prisoner. "Just what we need—a nice laurel crown for our Mr King!"

Affa placed the thorny crown on the prisoner's head very gently at first, but when it was in position, he pressed it down roughly, making the horrendous thorns press deeply into the man's head. Blood poured down his face and neck from the wounds the improvised crown had made. Once again, the prisoner winced in pain but said nothing in response to Affa's gratuitous cruelty. We squaddies were all laughing; somebody called Affa a cruel rat but laughed all the same. TJ disappeared outside and came back with a long reed. "Here's your sceptre Milord," he said, handing the man the reed and laughing as he held it as if it were a real sceptre. Dess was in front of the man now bowing in mock adoration before getting back to his feet and standing nose to nose with the prisoner.

“People like you make me sick, causing trouble and giving us hassle all the time. I’d crucify the lot of you if it were up to me,” he said harshly to the man before hitting him full in the face with the back of his hand. “That’s what I think of Jew Kings!” he jeered as he wiped the man’s blood from his hand. More soldiers had come in to witness the flogging and were now standing around laughing. A group of them who were off duty, and had had a few drinks strolled over, and started to taunt him. Someone said he was supposed to be a prophet, so one of them blindfolded him and told him to prophesy where the next punch was going to come from as they each took turns at hitting and punching him. The man was now hardly able to stand and stooped with the pain from the flogging and from the thorns piercing his head, as well as the pain inflicted by my taunting comrades.

“Attention,” shouted Affa suddenly and we all leapt to attention as Procurator Pilate walked into the room. It was the first time we had ever seen Pilate in our Guardroom, and he had taken us all by surprise. Unsmiling, he slowly walked over to the prisoner, paying particular attention to the purple robe, the sceptre and the thorny crown on his head. He looked at Affa.

“Who’s responsible for this?” he asked, stony faced.

“Just the lads having a bit of fun, Sir,” Affa replied.

Pilate silently looked round at us all for a long minute; we all held our breath, certain that he was going to explode with rage. He looked back once more at the prisoner then turned towards the doorway. “Bring him up to me,” he said as he left the room.

Affa snatched the reed from the man’s hand and threw it to one side. Luce tried to take the crown off the prisoners head. He swore as one of the thorns pierced a finger. "Leave it, leave it," said Affa, "he's seen it now!" Looking at Luce and TJ he said, "You two bring him upstairs with me. The rest of you, be ready to move when we come back down."

"Prisoner escort, quick march!" he barked as the group marched off to Pilate's office.

The Guardroom quickly emptied as the soldiers who weren't on duty melted away, worried that Pilate might come back again, and soon, only members of our contubernium were left.

"Phew, I thought we were all for it then," said Dess as we all relaxed once more.

"Trust Affa to blame us!"

"What do you think will happen to the prisoner now?" I asked him.

"I reckon, he'll get the chop," he replied dispassionately.

"Yeah," said Porky, sitting down in the corner and resting his feet on an upturned water bucket, "We'll soon be on our way to Gotha!"

Chapter 6

The road to Golgotha wound its way through the narrow crowded streets of the city, then out through Sheep's Gate and on beyond the city walls. The name, Golgotha, was Hebrew for "The Place of the Skull." And the parched dry area had been used as a place of public execution ever since Roman forces had first started to occupy Jerusalem. For the locals, it was a chilling place and had a sinister feel about it, and even to us, it had an aura and even a smell of pain, suffering and death. Condemned criminals would be forced to carry the crossbeam to which they would eventually have their hands nailed, from the barracks prison in Jerusalem through the streets and out of the City limits to Golgotha. Crowds would jeer and laugh as they passed in the street, and their humiliation was made worse by the fact that at Golgotha, they were stripped naked before being nailed to the cross. The very name, Golgotha, filled people with fear and for this reason, we lads used to call it "Gotha," as though it were a pet name for a place we really enjoyed visiting.

Gotha was fully equipped for crucifixions. It had scaffoldings with six substantial vertical wooden uprights and lifting beams with pulley blocks high above them. A wooden wedge-shaped footrest could be moved up or down the lower part of each upright to accommodate the stature of the prisoner, and behind the scaffolding was a heavy locked wooden box containing all the apparatus of crucifixion. There were hammers of different weights and sizes, wedges, pry bars and heavy iron nails of different lengths and thicknesses. There were also leather aprons, sponges, a leather carrying case and several pairs of heavy leather gloves. There was another smaller wooden box there too, and in this were kept metal mugs, leather water bottles and wineskins and a glazed earthenware bottle of Myrrh mixed with wine which was used as a mild anaesthetic to help deaden prisoners' pain. Also, in this box were materials for making a fire to stave off the evening chill for the benefit of the execution squad—not the prisoners. There were a number of hard wooden stretchers leaning up behind the scaffolding, together with a 'Longjohn'—a spear with a shaft almost three times the length of a normal spear—and a 'Legbreaker'—a heavy iron bar with hemp bindings round one end to act as a grip-handle. The Longjohn was used to stab prisoners in order to verify death after crucifixion. The Legbreaker was, as its name suggests, simply for breaking prisoners' legs. At the entrance to the execution site was the 'Shack'—a shelter for the use of the execution party in which we left our personal equipment and in which we were able to shelter in poor weather. All the crucifixion equipment was left there permanently at Golgotha, this 'Place of the Skull' which was used by all the Roman execution squads in Jerusalem.

The man had been taken by Affa and the escort to Pilate. Soon, we heard Pilate addressing the crowd which had assembled outside in the main quadrangle. It was difficult to hear what he was saying, but we recognised his voice and could tell he was debating with the crowd. He seemed to be asking them what he should do with the prisoner. To us, this was an unusual situation as Pilate always made his decisions on his own assessment of the situation and brooked no interference, very seldom even asking anyone for advice. He soon had his answer, however, as we heard the crowd at first shouting then chanting, "crucify, crucify, crucify!"

"What did I tell you?" said Dessie with a scowl, angrily throwing down the dice he had been toying with, "More donkey work for us!"

About ten minutes later, Affa and the escort arrived back with the prisoner.

"Come on lads, we've got an execution to do. Let's get on with it. The sooner we start, the sooner we get finished."

"Are you the Gotha squad?" said a voice from the doorway. A senior member of the Temple Guard was speaking to Affa.

"Why?" was Affa's gruff response.

"We've got two more here for you, both for crucifixion."

Affa swore, "Is there no one else on duty today? Why are we doing everything?"

The Temple Guardsman shrugged, "I've just been told to deliver them to you. Don't stab the messenger!"

He turned and shouted back through the doorway to his squad, and three more Temple Guards appeared escorting two filthy bloodied and dishevelled men in chains.

"You only just made it. We have to be going now," said Affa, making his mark against the paperwork proffered by the Temple Guard.

"Good luck!" said the Temple Guard Officer as he and his men left.

We took all three of the prisoners out into the yard. Our man still had on his crown, so once again, Luce tried to pull it off. It was firmly lodged on the man's head, secured into his flesh by the long thorns which were so profuse that Luce once again stabbed his hand in the attempt to remove it.

"Sorry, mate," he said, sucking his injured finger, "You'll have to keep it on. I'm certainly not going to try getting it off any more anyway!"

In the yard, we sorted out three suitably-sized wooden crossbeams. The prisoners would have to carry these to Gotha, normally across their backs. They would have their arms outstretched and their wrists tied to each end of the crossbeam. At Gotha, they would be laid on to the crossbeams and then the agony of crucifixion would start as their wrists were nailed to them. Then they would be hauled up using block and tackle and the crossbeam lodged into a notch on the main wooden upright. But all that was still to come.

Normally at a crucifixion, each prisoner would be allocated three soldiers of the execution squad, with one man in front to liaise with a Cavalryman who rode at the head of the procession to force a way through the crowd. As there were only six of us, plus Affa, to escort and execute three prisoners, Affa allocated just two men to each. Luce and Cass were allocated to the first man, Porky and TJ to the third one, and I was detailed to assist Affa with the second prisoner. Dess was allocated to front point liaison. By being in the middle of the three, Affa was able to keep his eye on what was happening throughout the procession. By chance, our prisoner happened to be the 'king', still wearing his thorny crown.

Although we weren't expecting trouble, we were fully armed. And one of each pair of soldiers held a short whip with which he could use on the prisoners if they were being belligerent or weren't moving quickly enough.

Soon, the grim procession started. Apart from the occasional jeer from some parts of the crowd, the general populace fell quiet as we passed them. And all we could hear was the incessant shouting by the Cavalryman at the front, of the only Hebrew word he knew—"Hazyz!" meaning "Move!" enabling him to force his way through the crowds. The first prisoner, under Luce's control, was fractious right from the start. Cursing us and everyone else, he refused to move until Cass kicked him and Luce used the whip on him. Then, struggling under the weight of his wooden crossbeam, he started to move. Once he got moving, he seemed to calm down and moved resignedly on and into the busy narrow streets where the local populace moved aside to let our grizzly parade through.

Our man, the "king," was by now exhausted with the flogging, the pain from the crown of thorns and the weight of the crossbar on his back. He struggled even to get to his feet, and both Affa and I had to take the weight of the crossbeam to allow him to stand up. As he started to walk forward, we gradually lowered the crossbeam until he was taking all its weight, and then we moved off, following Luce and Cass with their prisoner.

Our man was soon panting and groaning under the weight of the crossbeam, and I began to wonder if he would even survive the walk to Gotha.

"Is he going to make it?" I asked Affa.

"He'll be ok," Affa replied, but the look on his face told me that Affa himself wasn't sure he wouldn't die on the road to the execution site.

By now, the first group was quite a distance in front of us. Their prisoner was obviously a younger and stronger man than ours, and although he too had been flogged, he certainly didn't look in as bad shape as our man. Our prisoner was gasping for breath, sweating profusely and obviously in trouble. He wasn't going to make it, and I wasn't surprised when he fell heavily to his knees. Because his hands were tied to the wooden crossbeam, he was unable to support himself as he fell, and his face hit the floor and was bruised and bloodied even more than before.

"Come on, lad, nearly over now," said Affa in Hebrew, in an uncharacteristic display of sympathy as we tried to get the man back to his feet.

"This is no good," Affa continued. Then, looking towards the crowd of onlookers, he shouted in Hebrew.

"Hey you—yes you. You look like a strong chap, get this crossbar on your shoulder."

The tall muscular black man was taken aback when he realised that Affa was speaking to him. He tried to protest but he knew as well as Affa did that a Roman soldier could, by law, commandeer anyone other than a Roman Citizen to do his bidding. Affa untied the prisoner's wrists as the black guy and I took the weight of the crossbeam. He wiped the prisoner's face with a wet cloth he took from his leather pouch and helped him to his feet as we managed to get the crossbeam over the black man's shoulder. He carried it easily, but then…he hadn't been flogged to within an inch of his life.

Soon, we were on our way again. The third group were right behind us, so Affa was eager to get moving as quickly as possible, and was prodding our prisoner with his whip. Even without the crossbeam on his back, the prisoner struggled to walk, stumbling often until eventually, he fell once again. At the time, Affa had gone back to speak to the third group to tell them our man was struggling and to slow them down to give us some room. My attention was diverted as I was shouting at the black guy to tell him to wait for us. By now, he was quite a way in front of us. When I turned my attention back to the prisoner, I saw that a small group of women was helping him to his feet, wiping his face, giving him water to drink. He was trying to speak to them as they did so, his voice hoarse, every word seeming to be a struggle.

"Come on, get back!" shouted Affa fiercely at the women when he came back. "What are you doing, letting them get so close," he bawled at me. Without waiting for a response, he roughly grabbed the prisoner's arm and virtually dragged him back onto his feet, then lashed his back with the whip and kicked out at him to make him move. By now, the small display of sympathy had evaporated because Affa was concerned to get the procession to Gotha as soon as possible and before any other incident occurred.

By the time we reached Golgotha, Cass and Luce had their man up on the scaffold. He was still shouting and cursing them; Cass told us he had punched the prisoner in the face because as he was nailing the man's wrists to the crosspiece, the man had spit in his face. Affa and I were struggling with our prisoner because he was so weak and Affa wanted him on the cross before he died. It was a serious offence for a Roman execution squad to have a prisoner die before he was nailed to the cross.

To add to their humiliation in front of both male and female onlookers, prisoners were always crucified naked, so when the black guy laid the crossbeam down in front of the scaffolds we stripped our prisoner and then laid him on it, his arms outstretched.

"Hold his fingers flat," said Affa to me. Cass was standing by us with the hammer and a long iron nail in his hands.

"Get a nail in here," said Affa to him, pointing to our prisoner's wrist. Cass told me to press the man's arm against the wood and not to let him move.

"And if this one spits at me, he'll know about it!" he said.

He put the nail point against the man's wrist and drew back his arm before delivering a heavy blow which thrust the nail completely through the wrist and deep into the wood. The man cried out in pain as blood spurted from the wound. Cass was swinging the hammer back again to deliver another blow to ensure the nail had penetrated the wood far enough when the man spoke. I didn't hear what he said as my attention had been diverted to a woman in the crowd who had screamed out and buckled to her knees as she had witnessed the nail going through the man's wrist. I found out later that it had been the prisoner's mother. Cass's hand fell to his side, a look of incredulous disbelief on his face.

"Come on," shouted Affa, "get on with it!"

"…I can't…," stuttered Cass, "…he just said…I can't boss…"

"Give me them," said Affa as he roughly snatched the hammer and the nails from Cass and moved to the prisoner's other hand.

"Pull yourself together Sentius, or you will be on a charge when we get back to barracks," he shouted.

Cass didn't reply. Still obviously upset by what the man had said, he turned and walked away from us. "I've had enough of this…I've had enough," he said quietly.

Affa soon had the prisoner nailed to the crosspiece, and he and I looped the lifting ropes round each end of it.

"OK, up she goes!" shouted Affa to Dess, who was sitting astride the top cross member of the scaffold, rigging the sheave blocks ready for the lift. He threw the ropes down to us and we started to haul the prisoner up the scaffold until the crosspiece was almost level with the notch in the upright.

"Just a touch more," shouted Dess and then we heard the thud as the two pieces of the cross locked together. As Dess hammered a wedge in to ensure the two sections of the cross did not come apart, Affa started to slide the foot wedge up the lower half of the heavy upright.

"Here lad, hold his legs up a bit," he said to me. I took hold of the man's legs by his calves and took his weight.

"Bend his knees a bit," said Affa, and as I did so, he butted the foot wedge up against the soles of the man's feet and hammered in another wedge to hold it in position. Affa was sweating profusely by now and breathing heavily.

"I hope you're learning all of this," he said, turning to me as he wiped the sweat off of his forehead, "because I'm getting too old for this game. You can be in charge next time!" He felt in the leather pouch he had taken from Cass and drew out a double length iron nail.

"Now then, there's an art in this," he said to me. He put one of the prisoner's feet on top of the other then positioned the nail point in the centre of the prisoner's top foot. He suddenly jabbed it into the flesh, before delivering a heavy blow to the nail head with his hammer. The prisoner cried out in pain as the nail passed through both feet and penetrated the foot wedge.

"If you jab it in like that, it doesn't skid off sideways when you hit it. It goes in nice and smoothly." With a wry smile, he added, "more humane, you see. Ha-ha!"

The man was by now so near to death that he was passing in and out of consciousness, his body trying to protect him from the pain. I looked up and I have to confess to some sort of pity…he was obviously wracked in pain, bleeding from head, hands and feet, and staring death in the face. Affa had moved down to help with the third prisoner and called me to help too. With the extra help, we soon had him up on the cross too. And the hardest part of our task was complete.

Dess was still astride the top cross member when a Runner arrived from the barracks.

"I've been told to give you this," he said, holding out a rolled parchment to Affa. Affa unrolled it and looked at the two pages. Turning towards Dess, he shouted up, "Stay where you are, lad. I've another job for you!" Then he rolled the second page of parchment together with a couple of short nails round the hammer shaft and secured them with a length of hemp twine. He threw them up to Dess.

"Nail it above his head," he said, nodding towards our 'king' prisoner in the centre of the three.

"What's it say?" asked TJ.

"It says he's the king of the Jews," said Affa, "Pilate obviously wants these Jews to know what happens to kings inside the Roman Empire. They don't last long!" He laughed once more and turned to the crowd. Pointing to the notice, he shouted to them in Hebrew, "Make sure you remember that!"

At crucifixions, the crowd of onlookers was always kept well away from the scaffold. They had to remain behind a flimsy wooden barrier several metres from the foot of the crosses. There was quite a large crowd to watch the nailing and raising up of the condemned men, but as time went on, many drifted away. One of the lads explained that some of them would come back later to watch the prisoners die. But for us, it was a long boring affair with nothing to do but wait, and maybe play the odd game of dice whilst listening to the moaning and cursing of the dying men and the wailing and crying of their friends and relatives. The only two perks of the job were that we were allocated a day off after the execution, and that we were allowed to share out all of the prisoners' possessions. These, however, usually amounted to very little and consisted mainly of poor quality clothing and a little cash. Generally, these possessions were shared out equally, but we found that one piece of clothing which had belonged to our 'king' prisoner was highly sought after. It was an expensive outer garment, very well made and really quite stylish. We did think of tearing it apart by the seams and using the cloth to have some good quality shirts made, but then we realised it was woven in one piece without seams. And if we try and tear it or cut it would spoil the cloth. Luce suggested we draw lots for it, so he found some pieces of straw, cut one shorter than the rest, and we drew lots for it. Cass refused to be involved; in fact, he had been very quiet and withdrawn since the nailing incident. Dess won the draw and gloated at the rest of us as he folded the garment up and put it with his leather pouch in the shack.

Time passed very slowly. The sky had clouded over and it became quite dark and cold. We had lighted a fire in the brazier. And when the embers started to die away, I got up to get some more wood to throw on it. I noticed that Cass had wandered back to the scaffolds and was staring up at the ‘king’ on the cross. I had become a little concerned about him and walked up beside him.

“You OK, mate?” I asked.

Cass turned and looked at me for a long minute without speaking.

“Not really,” he said at last. “I’m beginning to wonder what it’s all about,” he went on. I was a little confused. I didn’t know what he meant and I guess he realised.

“That guy spat on my face as I nailed him to his cross,” he said, pointing to the first prisoner. “Him,” he pointed to our “king,” “he said he forgave me. He said he forgave us all actually. He said we didn’t know what we were doing. He’s probably right as well. That really stopped me in my tracks. I could have understood it, could have dealt with it, if he had spat in my eye too. But to forgive me…that really got to me. It’s really made me think.”

I had no response. I too couldn’t understand why anyone would want to forgive someone who was causing them so much pain.

“You know,” Cass went on, “I’m beginning to think, maybe, he is someone special after all. Maybe he really is a king or something,” he said with a shrug, “He’s certainly different from anyone else I’ve ever had to deal with.”

I put my hand on his arm to try to give him some support, “No, mate, I don’t get it either. Maybe you’re right…”

“I’ve had enough of this barbarism,” said Cass, “I’ve just about had enough.” He walked to the back of the scaffolds and took hold of the Longjohn. Without speaking, he speared a sponge he had taken from his pouch, dipped it into the bowl containing the myrrh and wine potion, and held it up to the “king.” The man had been passing in and out of consciousness for some while and was very near to death now. Even so, he refused to drink it, wincing as he moved his head away from the wet sponge.

There had been an eerie silence for quite a while. The prisoners all seemed to have quietened, mainly because they were all by now only semi-conscious, while the friends and relatives who were still there were sitting quietly, waiting for the end, the women silently weeping. Our 'king' was the first to die. It was about mid-afternoon, but the sky had been clouding over for an hour or so. And it was now eerily dark and dismal, and it looked like we were in for a real downpour. Affa had sent me back to the Shack to get our foul weather clothing, and as I passed our "king," he had briefly regained consciousness and was, I thought, hallucinating and talking gibberish. Affa later explained to me that he had been shouting to his mother and others of his followers who were in the group behind the picket fence.

The rain started and I ran into the cover of the Shack and hurriedly collected our foul weather clothing, only stopping long enough to put mine on before running back to the rest of the squad who were now squatting down at the base of the scaffolds trying to shelter from the rain. By now, the sky was a purple black, the clouds were scudding wildly, and rain was pouring down worse than I'd ever seen it since I arrived in Judea.

There seemed no reason for us to stay out of the Shack; our 'king' had died by now, and the other two were not far from death, still slipping in and out of consciousness. So almost all of us ended up cramped together in the Shack; some of the lads playing dice, some just trying to relax as best they could before the hard work of taking the prisoners down from their crosses began. Only Cass was still in the execution area. Seemingly unaware of the torrential rain, he moodily wandered back and forth in front of the three prisoners, often stopping in front of our 'king' and looking up at him, before pensively moving away again. He was soaked, but didn't seem to care. Clearly, his mind was enduring some great emotional turmoil.

After another hour or so, the rain started to ease and the leaden sky lightened a little. Luce and Porky had gone into the main execution area to stretch their legs. Affa looked up at the sky. It was still raining a little, but he knew that if we didn't start clearing the site, complete darkness would make the job almost impossible.

"Come on, you idle lot, let's get this job wrapped up," he said.

Grudgingly, the squad stirred; Dess started dousing the embers of the fire as others started to put away the equipment not now needed. As we worked, the squeak of wooden axles and the sound of wheels on gravel made me turn in the direction of the roadway into Gotha. A toothless old Hebrew was seated on a flat cart being pulled along by an even older donkey.

"Who's this?" I asked Luce.

"Ha-ha, that's the Fire Man," he replied, "He's come to take away the bodies. He's paid by the Temple Authorities to take away the bodies and bury them because Jewish law says even criminals have to be properly buried. But all he does is burn them and pocket the cash. It's easier and cheaper to burn them than to dig graves!"

"There's a bloke here who wants to speak to you," said Dess to Affa, nodding towards a group of people standing together behind the picket fence. Affa looked over at the man, and then indicated he should come through the picket line. They stood talking quietly for a few minutes, then the man handed Affa a small leather bag, and went back to the group.

"Right," said Affa, putting the leather bag into his pouch and picking up the Longjohn, "Let's check 'em." With the Longjohn over his shoulder, he walked towards the first prisoner and put the point of the long spear against the man's naked chest. He prodded the man and he cried out in pain.

"Right," he said, "He needs breaking, Dess." He walked to the next man, our 'king', and did the same. The man didn't make any sound at all so Affa pushed the spear deep into the man's side. Blood and what appeared to be water started to bleed out of the wound but still the man made no sound.

"He's had it," said Affa, moving towards the next man.

"Why is he bleeding water?" I asked Dess who was walking back towards the first prisoner with the Legbreaker over his shoulder.

"Affa's just stabbed him to see if he could get a reaction, to see if he is still alive. He must have pierced a lung because when they crucify you, your lungs fill up with a sort of watery stuff and you asphyxiate, that's what eventually kills you. That's why they keep trying to push upwards with their feet to take the weight off their arms so they can breathe. That's why I'm going to break this one's legs to stop him pushing up. Then he'll soon die."

"Break his legs?" I asked, wide eyed.

"Yeah, watch," said Dess as he swung the heavy bar behind his head and aimed it at the prisoner's shin bones. The man screamed out in pain as, with a sickening crack, the bar broke his bones. Dess was completely unmoved by his actions and of the pain he had inflicted on the prisoner, and was wiping the bar with a cloth he had had tucked into his belt. "Gotta wipe it," he said with a grin, "to make sure it doesn't skid off when I hit the next bloke's legs!"

He stood in front of our 'king' and swung the Legbreaker back. Before he smashed the bar against the man's legs, Affa stopped him.

"Don't waste your strength; I just said he's had it!" he said, wagging his finger as usual, "You want to try listening sometimes!"

Dess walked down to the third man and carried out his gruesome task. Whilst the other two men were in their last moments of life, gasping and struggling to breathe, we set about taking down our "king." This time Luce was on the high cross member of the scaffold, and he reached out to catch the lifting ropes which were being thrown up to him. He soon had them looped over the wooden crossbeam and threaded round the pulley blocks. He threw the loose ends down to us. We started to pull on them. As we took the man's weight, Luce knocked out the wedge and kicked the crosspiece away from the upright. The man's weight and the wooden baulk were very heavy and it took three of us to lower him to the ground. Dess got to work with a nail bar removing the nails from the man's hands and feet, and as he did so, the toothless old Fire-Man shuffled towards us with a wooden stretcher in his hands.

"No, not this one," said Affa, "He's spoken for. Leave the stretcher here."

Luce and Dess looked at each other in disbelief.

"What's that about?" Luce asked Affa.

"I've made an arrangement with his family," said Affa, "They want to bury him themselves." He turned towards the group at the picket fence and beckoned them towards the corpse of our "king." They quickly came forward; obviously worried that Affa might change his mind now that he had his payoff.

"Come on," said Affa to us, "Leave 'em to it."

As we moved away, I watched the men cover the hard wooden stretcher with blankets while the women, still quietly weeping, tenderly wiped away the sweat, dirt and blood from the man's face and covered his body with a loincloth in an attempt to preserve some dignity. Then the men lifted him onto the stretcher, carefully, as if he were still alive and they wanted to prevent him from any more pain. They covered him with another blanket as the oldest woman of the party protected her hands with folded cloths, then gently pulled the crown of thorns from the man's head and, with a look of disgust and contempt on her face, threw it onto the roadway. It landed in a puddle and as I watched, the Fire Man's cart wheel rolled over it as he moved from the gateway of the execution site to the end of the scaffold. Soon, the men in the party lifted the stretcher and the sad little procession made its way down the roadway leading away from Golgotha.

As I walked back towards the other two prisoners, Affa handed me the Longjohn to put away.

"Come on, lads," he said, "let's get to it!"

Chapter 7

We all slept well that night; the work had been hard, even harder than usual the lads told me because we were so short staffed. Still, I thought, I had experienced my first crucifixion. And though I hadn't particularly enjoyed it in the way that some of the other lads had seemed to have, I did feel that I had handled it ok.

The day following the crucifixion was for us a rest day, so we spent our time relaxing, writing letters home, lying in the sun, swimming, and generally enjoying ourselves. It was the Jewish Sabbath, their main religious day in the week, so we knew there would be relative peace and quiet, and we were less likely to have our rest day interrupted to provide back-up for squads trying to keep order in the city. But later, our contentedness took a knock when we learned that we had been detailed to a night duty job, guarding the tomb of one of the men we had crucified. The trial and crucifixion of our 'king' had caused a lot of trouble for the Temple Dignitaries, because his followers had put about the story that within three days of his death, he would miraculously come back to life. Although everyone knew this was impossible, they were concerned that his body might be stolen and that his followers would then say that he had indeed come back to life. Pilate had reluctantly agreed to deploy a squad to the cemetery area in order to guard the tomb. And Centurian Isauricus, our commanding officer, had decided that as we had just had a rest day, we would be suitably refreshed to do the job. Affa did his best to get us out of it, reminding the Centurian that we had been the execution squad. The response had been simple and to the point. "Excellent. You executed him—Now you can finish the job!"

On the good side, besides the rest day, we had most of the following day off too because we weren't deployed until dusk. All too quickly, however, the time arrived for us to deploy to the cemetery, which was located a fair distance outside the city wall.

"We'll split the shift," said Affa as we went through the cemetery gateway, "half of us on watch, the other half can have a kip. No-one will be checking up on us tonight. Half way through the shift, we'll change over. I'll look after the first shift. Luce, you're in charge of the second shift. Take half the squad and bed down."

While we set up camp and got a fire going, Affa and Luce went up to the tomb to check it out. By the time they came back, we had just about got everything organised.

"All ok?" Dess asked Affa.

"Oh yeah," he replied, "Nobody's gonna get in or out of there! There's a massive great stone blocking the entrance, and it has been sealed and grouted round the edge and bottom with earth and stones and tamped down really well. They've made a good job of it. It would take a dozen blokes to move it! I think we can rest easy tonight, lads! A cushy number for a change," he said, smiling.

From our duty campsite, we could see the tomb entrance quite clearly; some of us went to have a closer look at it and it was, as Affa had said, virtually impregnable. We couldn't understand why we even needed to be there. It was obvious to us that there was not the slightest chance of anyone being able to get into the tomb and steal the body.

Night drew in. It was a cold night, and those of us who were on second watch were glad to be able to turn in and keep warm under the horse blankets we had brought with us. We had lighted a second fire a good way from the main campsite, so we could have warmth with our bit of peace and quiet. But from this secondary campsite, we couldn't see the tomb or even the main campsite. Soon, we were snoring peacefully.

I was woken up half way through the night by TJ. By now, the night was really cold, and the fire had begun to die down. We got ourselves organised, rekindled the fire for the benefit of Affa's shift, and then made our way wearily towards the duty campsite. The fire there was blazing vigorously, and TJ and I squatted down to warm ourselves. We heard Luce and Dess coming up behind us to join us ready to relieve Affa and his watch.

"What's up there?" said Luce, looking past Affa towards the tomb we were guarding.

"Why?" said Affa, turning languidly to see what Luce was staring at.

"All the gods!" he suddenly exclaimed, almost choking on his drink and suddenly jumping to his feet. The tomb we were supposed to be guarding was wide open; the stone had been moved a good two metres away from the entrance. And it even looked as if the soil and gravel which previously had been used to seal around the edges had been shovelled well out of the way too. Affa was running towards the tomb entrance.

"Spread out, spread out!" he shouted over his shoulder, "Search the whole area. They can't have got far!"

Fortunately, there was bright moonlight to help us, and we were able to quickly search the whole of the small cemetery area. Finding nothing, we ran back towards the tomb and met Affa coming away from it.

"What's the score?" said Dess.

"Nothing inside except a grave cloth," said Affa, breathing heavily. He looked ashen; I had never before seen such a look of fear and anxiety on his face.

"I only went up to have a look around about half an hour ago. Everything was secure, I swear it!" he said. Porky confirmed it and Affa went on, "Anything out there? Anyone see anything? Any tracks or anything?"

None of us had seen a thing. Everything was still and silent; no signs of movement, no signs that there had been any kind of movement for hours.

"All the gods," said Affa, "We're in big trouble now! We'll be the next ones nailed to crosses at Gotha!"

"What are we gonna do?" someone said. By now, I felt physically sick, as though I had been kicked in the stomach, knowing that the punishment for sleeping on duty was death. And just having witnessed at such close quarters the kind of death I would have to endure, I, like all my mates, was panic-stricken.

"Can't we just say someone overpowered us and stole the body?" said Dess.

"Are you mad!" shouted Affa in desperation, "You get the chop for sleeping on duty, you get the chop for losing a prisoner like this; whichever way we go, we're dead men. Dead men!" he repeated, as if he needed to emphasise the gravity of our situation.

I looked around. All my comrades were sickened and scared at the prospects we faced.

"Listen, we've got to get away from here!" said Affa as he started to regain his composure and take command of the situation.

"What—desertion? Man, things are going from bad to worse, that's another thing punishable by death!!! Oh man, what are we going to do?" said Dess, running his hands nervously through his hair.

"Listen," said Affa once more, "We're dead men whatever we do. The only chance we have now is to get away from here. If we move now, we can make good headway before anyone even knows we're gone. Nobody's gonna relieve us; they're only expecting us back at barracks at mid-morning. At least if we run now, we've got a chance. If we don't, we're dead men, dead men!"

There was little reaction. We all knew he was right.

"Everybody ok with it? I need everybody with me," said Affa. None of us were happy about the prospect of desertion but we all realised it was the only thing we could do to save our lives. No one dissented and so, we all started hurriedly to get our things together and prepare to go. Cass, however, sunk to his knees and stared vacantly onto the ground in front of himself.

"Come on!" shouted Affa when he noticed that Cass was the only man not preparing to go.

"We can't do this," said Cass, "It's not right. We should just be honest, and go back to barracks, and tell them we found the tomb empty and the body gone. There's something special about this 'king' bloke…I think we'll be alright if we just tell the truth."

Affa was incensed. "Are you mad, man?" he raged. "Someone's nicked the body! They must have found a back way into the tomb or something. I don't know how they've done it, but they have! The bloke was dead; we crucified him, I stabbed him with the Longjohn. I saw him die! He was stone dead! We *all* saw him die! Somebody, somehow, has stolen his body!"

"Maybe we should have broken his legs as well as the other two…" said Dess.

"He was DEAD! I made *sure* he was dead. What's the matter with you all? It's my responsibility to make sure they're dead before we get them down off the scaffold and I did. He was STONE DEAD!" shouted Affa in desperation.

"Yes but…he was special…" said Cass.

"Don't talk rubbish," Affa snapped, "People don't come back to life. When you're dead, you're dead, and that's an end to it. Is he some kind of magician or something? Listen, you've been wandering about like a lovesick teenager all day. What's up with you? Get a grip, man. Get your things together and let's get going. The longer we stand around arguing, the more likely we are to be caught and crucified ourselves!"

Affa stomped away from him and started getting himself organised but by the time we were all ready to go, Cass still hadn't moved.

With a deep sigh, Affa walked back over to him and put his arm around Cass's shoulders. In spite of his obvious frustration, he suddenly seemed more understanding of Cass's feelings.

"Ok lad, ok," he said with a sigh, "Come on up to the top end of the cemetery and lets have a quick natter. We all feel that we have to go. If you're going to stay, I don't want you to tell them which direction we are going in, ok?" They walked steadily away from us. "If you want to stay, that's your business. I accept that and respect you for it..." Affa went on. I was unable to hear much else of what Affa said to him. And soon, they were out of sight at the far end of the cemetery. Nervously and anxiously, we waited for Affa.

"Come on, Affa," said Luce quietly to himself, "We gotta be off, we gotta be off..."

At last, Affa appeared out of the gloom, walking briskly towards us alone.

"What's happening now?" asked Dess.

"He's staying here," said Affa, "Come on," he added, "we're wasting precious time."

Chapter 8

By the time dawn had started to break, we had travelled a good distance. Our original intention had been to travel at night only, but now we knew that we needed to put as much distance between us and Jerusalem as possible, as quickly as we could. We also knew that no-one would be aware of our absence until around mid-morning, so we still had time on our side. We kept on going into daylight hours, not stopping for anything, even food or drink. We had plenty of cash between us, and in any case, we knew we could live off the land if necessary, so we had no worries about food and drink. But at that stage, no-one felt like eating; all we wanted to do was to get away as fast as possible. We had tried to disguise our uniforms as much as we could, turning tunics inside out, putting our undershirts on over the top of them and covering our armoured kilts with our cloaks. It was not too convincing, but was the best we could do. And in any case, we were determined to keep well away from any other travellers. In Roman fashion, we were all clean shaven, so we pulled our cloaks around our mouths and the bottom part of our faces so as not to look so distinctively Roman. When we first left the cemetery area, we wrapped our feet with items of our clothing in an attempt to make tracking difficult, and used a leafy tree bough to sweep away tracks behind us. We went out of our way to find water to wade through in order to destroy any scent because we thought pursuers would probably use dogs to track us. We kept away from all roadways, going overland and travelling south rather than west towards the Mediterranean coast because Affa felt that west was the way we would be expected to go. His plan was to travel south east and follow the coast of the Dead Sea before crossing the Jordan and travelling out of Judea and into Peria.

Peria was a barren and inhospitable province of Palestine, which, at that time, was very sparsely populated. Most of the inhabitants of Peria lived in small townships where valleys made agriculture possible, or in Garrison outpost towns. Travelling at night and keeping well away from such townships, our intention was to go west into the foothills of the Peria Mountains, and then finally north through the mountains themselves, hoping eventually to move towards the coast of the Mediterranean many miles north of Jerusalem in order to find a ship which would take us off the mainland and away to safety. That was Affa's plan. Looking back, I suppose it was very ambitious, but we trusted Affa implicitly. He knew the language; he knew the country; and most of all he knew the consequences of us being caught, as did the rest of us.

It was late in the day by the time we all started showing signs of fatigue, so we slowed and finally stopped to rest. Porky, because of his build, was particularly exhausted.

We stopped at an area which was deserted but had a little clear water pool. The water was very welcome to both drink and to cool us.

"What are we going to do, Boss?" said Dess.

"We'll have to get a boat away from the mainland…maybe get to Cyprus or even further away if we can; somewhere Rome doesn't care too much about. But I reckon, they will expect us to go to the nearest Mediterranean port, maybe Joppa or somewhere like that. That's why we have to go the long way round and that's why we need to go in the opposite direction first to confuse anybody chasing us."

"Will they send someone after us then?" I asked nervously.

"Oh yeah," said Luce, "You can count on it! They'll track us, probably using professional trackers and maybe dogs. They'll send fast dispatch riders to local ports and townships to get other garrisons to look out for us. They'll want to show the rest of the blokes that you can't just go AWOL and think they will forget about you."

"Listen, lads," said Affa. "We have to be careful. If anybody still has any bits of uniform—you for example," he said, looking at me and pointing to my uniform belt, "Get rid of it now. You need to bury it. Don't forget, Rome wants us, the Zealots will kill us, and the ordinary populace will betray us; nobody wants to help us. We have to look out for each other, and trust NOBODY else."

I got up and took off my uniform belt. Scraping away the sand, I made a deep hole and buried it. Then I returned to the rest of the lads. Affa threw me a length of hemp twine he had fished out of his leather pouch.

"Here," he said. "We don't want you losing your britches lad!" he said with a wan smile.

By now, I was privately wondering if we had done the right thing. But when I considered again the alternatives—being murdered by Zealots or crucified by Pilate, I knew that we had to trust Affa to get us as far away as possible as soon as possible.

When we were rested, we decided to press on, still concerned to keep well in front of whoever might be chasing us. Affa seemed to know the country well, and even though he had said we must be careful, we now needed food and he felt sure that if we could find some nomadic shepherds or goatherds, he may be able to buy some instead of having to try to find and kill our own, which would slow us down. He had a good command of the language, and when eventually we saw, through the semi-darkness, a campfire, he told us to keep watch, keep quiet, and keep out of sight.

He took Luce and they went together towards the camp area. We could hear them talking, the shepherds seemed to be amenable and we watched as Affa handed over money in exchange for two large bags of food. Affa and Luce took a circuitous route to get back to us, and then we all moved quietly away to make a temporary camp simply to rest and eat, well away from the goatherds. Straight after the meal, we packed away the remnants of the food, then struck camp and started to move on, again concerned that we keep well in front of anyone might be searching for us. In any case, we were all too anxious and nervous to rest; adrenaline was driving us and so we moved quickly on into the night.

That was the way we existed in those first days and weeks on the run, continually living on our nerves, always looking over our shoulders, starting at any unusual sounds, hiding if we saw a cloud of dirt in the distance in case it should be Roman Cavalry. Eventually, we began to relax a little, we started to feel that maybe we would get away after all, that maybe Pilate didn't care that we had deserted. We knew we were a good distance from Jerusalem by now, and we had not seen any trace of anyone following us or searching for us. We had travelled mostly at night, always posting lookouts whenever we rested and had been lucky as far as food and water was concerned; having caught and killed a stray goat to supplement the food Affa had bought from the nomads. We had also managed to ration the water we had without it causing us any great hardship.

But it was hard work travelling regularly at night. It was bitterly cold. And as we were travelling overland to avoid roads and pathways, we often stumbled, cutting hands and feet on rocks, grazing our skin and stubbing our toes. Often, it was so cold that we would only realise we had cut or grazed ourselves when daylight came and the sun started to warm us up; that was when we started to feel the pain and the blood trickling down. It was pitch black too; difficult to see where we were going, even to see the man in front or behind. We moved in single file, following the tracks of the man in front, leaving the responsibility of finding the way to Affa, who was always in the lead. We tried to keep fairly close to each other but it was difficult; sometimes, a man would lag behind and the group would tend to split into two or more parts. Despite that, we were soldiers and used to forced marches. And we stuck it out with confidence and determination. In the early hours of a particularly black, cold and miserable night, however, things took a more challenging turn.

I was almost at the rear of the column of men struggling along in the darkness. Suddenly, I heard Dess running up behind me.

"Tersh," he said quietly but urgently. From the anxiety in his voice, I knew there was a problem.

"Tell them to stop. I can't see Porky behind me!"

I passed the message up to Affa who was, as always, leading the column. And soon, we were congregating together.

"How long ago did you lose sight of him?" asked Affa.

"I spoke to him about half an hour ago and told him to keep up as I couldn't hear him at all and felt he had dropped too far back. I heard him shout that he was ok but he still seemed a fair way behind."

"We need to retrace our steps," said Affa, "And we need to keep together; we don't want to lose anyone else."

We silently retraced our steps but it was difficult; we couldn't really see for certain exactly where we had been, and we made several detours thinking we were walking in completely the wrong direction.

"This is hopeless," said Affa, "We'll soon be so lost that we'll never be able to find our way anywhere. We need to stop now and rest until daybreak. Then we will be able to pick up our tracks and follow them back. He can't have got far!"

We still didn't want to make a fire, especially at night, and because we were resting instead of walking, the bitter cold stiffened our limbs and made old scars hurt. We wrapped our cloaks and horse blankets around ourselves and huddled together to keep warm, and most of us managed a couple of hours sleep.

As the sky lightened, men started to get up, stamping their feet and swinging their arms as they tried to get their limbs working once more. Soon, everyone was up and eager to get started, so we shared some strips of jerky, dried goat's meat from the bags of food Affa had bought from the goatherds which we could eat as we walked along. We then started to retrace our steps, looking all the while for kicked-over sand, dislodged stones and rocks which indicated we had walked there in the opposite direction the night before.

Affa, always the professional soldier, had detailed Dess and TJ to walk at each side of the group and look out for problems in the distance whilst the rest of us scrutinised the ground for signs that we had travelled that way during the night. We had been following the tracks, going back over the area where we had walked during the night for more than an hour before we heard a shout from Dess. He had seen something lying in the scree and scrub up ahead. Affa told us to take cover and be prepared to engage if we had to, while he and Luce cautiously approached the object. We watched as they gingerly prodded and poked at the bundle, then saw Affa stand up and wave us over. We all ran over to where they were. It was Porky. He was dead, lying awkwardly and unnaturally on one side.

"Exhaustion? Hypothermia?" suggested Luce. Affa was silent. He moved Porky's clothing away from his lower legs.

"That's what's killed him," he said, pointing to two small puncture marks on his left leg just below the calf, "Snake bite!"

"Snake bite???"

"Aye—from the spacing of the fang marks, it looks like a Black Desert Cobra," Affa continued, pointing at the puncture marks around which the skin was a yellow-purple colour and badly swollen, "At least, the lad wouldn't have suffered for long. You go down pretty quick when one of them beggars takes a bite out of you!"

"Snake bite! What a way to go!" said TJ.

“This terrible, terrible country,” said Luce, “I’ll be glad to get away from it.”

“Well, these things happen,” said Affa with a sigh. “Right,” he continued, “Come on, lads, we need to quickly bury him and get moving. We can’t afford to hang around, we got to keep moving!”

Chapter 9

It was several days later when we had started to move east again and move away from the mountainous area and into an area of Peria which was a little less craggy and scabrous, and was easier to travel through. The problem we knew we might face now was the possibility of us coming across other travellers or worse, Roman soldiers. Our worst fears were realised early one morning when, after having travelled during a moonless night in the bitter cold, we were setting up camp to rest during the day. Luce, who had been doing a recce of the area came back and reported to Affa that he had heard noises and voices in an area just north of our position.

"I have a feeling it might be Romans," he told Affa with a worried expression on his face.

"Ok," said Affa. Turning to the rest of us, he said, "You lot keep quiet and get your heads down, this might be a search party looking for us." Then to Luce he said, "Me and you will have a closer look." Turning to me, he said, "You too, lad. You're the fittest of us, you can be the runner."

Exchanging worried glances, the rest of the lads looked for cover whilst the three of us started to make our way forward; bent double at first then on our bellies wriggling along like snakes; conscious that if we were seen or heard by anyone, it may well be the end of us all, and a very tortuous end it might be too.

We reached the top of a slight rise and could see a group of about twenty Roman soldiers busily setting up a field kitchen and camp some distance away. It didn't look as if they had set up any sort of picket line, and the soldier in charge seemed to be doing a lot of shouting at the men under him.

Affa wanted to get a little closer, so we once again wriggled our way over the slight ridge in front of us and moved forward to the cover of another escarpment. Carefully, we raised our heads above cover.

"Ummm…this is strange," Affa whispered, "Very strange…they look like a unit of greenhorns—the way they are performing…Yeah, they are getting some grief from the Tesserarius, the Guard Commander in charge of them ha-ha…"

He was quiet for a moment. Shielding his eyes from the low morning sun, he studied the group's leader.

"Hey, this is a bit of luck…I know this guy!" he whispered with a smile.

"You know him?" said Luce. "Is that good or bad then?"

"It's good, it's good…It's a guy called Albus Septimus—great bloke. We joined up together and went through basic training together. We joined the same unit and were best mates for a good few years. Eventually, the unit was dispersed and they sent me on a course to learn Hebrew, and then sent me here—he was promoted to Decanis in a training unit. I guess he's moved up in the world, been promoted, and put in charge of it now. I didn't know they had set up any training garrisons in this part of the world, though."

“Yeah, it’s all right talking about all our yesterdays, but it doesn’t help us any, does it?” said Luce.

“Get away, lad, it’s the best thing that could have happened. I’ll go have a quick chat with my old mate and we’ll be up and running!”

“What!!! You must be joking!” said Luce, trying to convey his incredulity and annoyance, whilst still remaining quiet and respectful to his boss. “We’re deserters, Boss—deserters. Even if he is your mate, he’ll be in trouble himself if he gets to know we’re here and he doesn’t arrest us and take us back. Man, I know they’re all greenhorns but there are some big lads there and a lot of them…I rate our chances of getting away as zero if they get to know we’re here!”

Affa smiled, “Listen, lad, have I ever let you down? I GUARANTEE we’ll be ok. You just leave it to me. And look, there’s the ideal opportunity for me to get right beside him!”

In the distance, we could see two figures: an old man and what looked like his Grandson driving a group of about fifteen goats towards the Roman encampment, obviously intending to try and sell some of the beasts. Affa wrapped his coat around himself against the light wind which had just sprung up and pulled his hood up over his head so that from a distance, he would look like just another goatherd. “Listen,” he said to us both, “If I wave my LEFT hand, you two run to the others and then get away as fast as you can ’cos that will mean trouble. But if I use my RIGHT hand, you can rest easy. OK?”

In a second, he was gone. And hardly before we knew it, he was to be seen trailing behind the last of the two goatherds. The sound of the camp being set up together with the sound of the goats and the fact that the light wind was blowing towards us, meant that the goatherds didn't hear him—didn't even realise he was with them. As the group reached the camp, Affa moved in front of them and went straight to the man in charge of the group of soldiers.

"What's happening?" I said to Luce as he peered over the edge of the ridge once again, "Is it left hand or right?" My heart was pounding in my chest, and I have to admit, I was really quite scared. I was convinced that within minutes, a group of these young recruits, eager to score points from their Boss, would be running towards us, armed to the teeth. And I knew we wouldn't stand a chance, however quickly we ran.

"Well blow me…" said Luce, "No hands at all for us mate; he's shaking hands with the guy in charge!"

"Really?"

"Yeah…man, I don't believe Affa, sometimes. I just don't know how he gets away with it! He's gone with his mate into the tent...oh wait. He's come back out again…Ha-ha, blow me. He's just come back out of the tent, waved his right hand, and gone back in again!"

Luce looked at me with a smile and shook his head. "That man," he said, "Thank all the gods, he's on our side!"

As I had been delegated to be runner, I went back to our unit and told the lads what had happened. All the guys were as dumbfounded as Luce and I had been. But I have to say, we were all relieved too. The running and the ever-present dust in the air had made me parched, so I had a drink and then started to make my way back to Luce. As I scrambled up the scree beside him, I asked if there had been any further developments. Luce was studying the scene before us once again.

"No change," he said, "But Affa has just come out of the tent with a big bag of loot and a smile on his face, and the greenhorns are starting to strike camp!" By now I was beside Luce looking over the edge of the escarpment, and I could see that tackle and equipment were being packed away. And I could see the unmistakeable squat heavy set figure of Affa walking away to our right.

"Where's he going now?" I asked.

"He'll be coming back here, but he won't want to give away where we are. He has a knack of getting people to trust him but he never trusts anyone himself!"

Affa was really upbeat when he got back to us, and after we had got back to the rest of the unit, he explained that not only had his friend given him food and drink, he had also given him cash and information.

"There isn't a general alert out for us after all, but he knows for certain that the Military Police has been on the lookout. They did take dogs to the cemetery but they weren't able to pick up a scent, so the MPs brought in Bedouin trackers to look for us. But when the Bedouins found out it was me they were chasing, they told Agapus that they couldn't find anything. I know loads of those blokes, and I've done a lot of business with them over the years. Seems like our friendship has paid off! The MPs spent time searching for us between Jerusalem and the near coast, and eventually put our case on the back burner. But we can't afford to get complacent, lads, because I've known similar situations before when they haven't said much on AWOL cases because they can't trust enlisted men not to cover for their mates. And apparently, they have conned some of the Temple Guard into confessing that they were on guard duty at the cemetery and that they were overpowered by a group of blokes who opened the grave and stole the body! They paid them off. But to be honest, I'd be surprised if they ever get to spend their money. Now, they have someone to blame; they will punish them. That's what I think anyway. Mind you, that would be better for us because they wouldn't want to find us then."

"The MPs will want to find us, you can depend on that," someone said. "Yeah, especially Agatopus," someone else added.

"Boss," said TJ, "I'm worried about this mate of yours; what if he splits on us…"

"No, no, he's sound, he won't shop us. But he did say that if we were intending to reach the coast and get away from the mainland, that Joppa and the surrounding area is crawling with troops, just as I thought. He says they are on a special exercise which could go on for some time but…well, they might be just looking for us."

"Oh no—how are we gonna get away from the mainland if troops are all over the coast?" said TJ.

"Don't worry lad—just trust me," said Affa, "By the time we get to the coast, we will be well away from any troops. We will be miles north of any military outposts."

"How are we going to get past your mate and his crew of rookies if they are just setting up camp, Boss?" asked Luce.

"They were only just setting up when I went to speak to him but he has got them packing down ready to move straight on now so that they will be out of our hair. He told them they were too slow getting themselves organised, so they have to move further on before they can have a meal!"

"Did you say you trained together?" said Luce with a sly grin, "It figures!"

Chapter 10

Resting during the heat of the day and travelling during the bitterly cold night was physically draining. As disciplined soldiers, used to forced marches, we were mentally as well as physically tough enough to cope. But with the added anxiety of literally running for our lives, it was only Affa's leadership and our sense of discipline which kept us going. We still posted lookouts during the daytime rest periods and always spent time looking for rest areas in which we could hide ourselves effectively. The cloudless skies always meant a bitterly cold night, and travelling across country rather than using roads and paths meant not only that it was heavy going, but also that we never encountered any other travellers in this dry, arid and unforgiving wilderness. As we travelled at night, we always travelled in single file with Affa at the front. Moonless nights were the worst. When it was pitch black, it was difficult to see the men in front or behind, even though the loss of Porky had made us conscious of the need to keep a close eye on each other.

It was on one such night when we encountered a scruffy but well-camouflaged campsite which Affa immediately guessed might be a Zealot encampment. They hadn't posted any picket lookouts, so it was easy for us to get close to them and take them by surprise. Still not quite sure it was Zealots, Affa decided we should approach them amicably. Led by Affa, we wandered casually into the encampment, our weapons concealed from view but readily to hand.

"Hello friends," said Affa, "we're nomadic merchants just passing through this area. I need to speak to someone. I have problems with some of my mules. Who is in charge?"

The men had all stood up nervously when we entered their campsite, looking anxiously at each other, their hands on the handles of their daggers.

"Wait here," said one of the men, unsmiling, "I'll get him." The other men seemed to relax a little when they realised we weren't intending to rob or attack them. In fact, they had now realised they outnumbered us. The man returned with another older well-built man. Silently, he looked us all up and down as he approached, then suddenly, as if he had noticed something of significance about us, he quickly started to draw his dagger as he shouted to his men.

"Romans!" he shouted. They all reacted immediately but we were all like coiled springs, and when we saw Affa move, we all leapt into action. As soon as he saw the man's reaction, Affa had drawn his dagger. And in one swift move he had stabbed the man closest to him before the man had time to react. Even before the first man hit the floor, Affa was attacking the leader of the group and we had all engaged too. We were outnumbered, but we were fighting for our lives, and were better armed, better trained, and had the element of surprise on our side. It was a violent and vicious skirmish, and I became locked in mortal combat with a strong athletic young guy who would, I'm sure, have overpowered me had Luce not attacked him from behind. As we started to overpower them, two of their group managed to break away from the fight and run off into the night. Luce and TJ gave chase and soon returned, both of them breathing heavily and wiping blood from the blades of their daggers.

"All ok?" said Affa.

"Yeah, we got 'em all," said TJ, "Is everyone here ok?"

"Looks like Dess took a hit," said Affa as he knelt down beside the injured soldier. Dess was on his knees; bending forward and clutching his stomach, moaning quietly.

TJ and Affa looked at his wound, a deep cut into his abdomen. He was losing blood profusely, and Affa set to work trying to stem the flow. TJ handed him medical supplies which we kept in our pouches, and soon, Dess was being helped to his feet.

"How you feeling mate?" said TJ. Dess nodded and hoarsely whispered, "Ok, yeah, not bad." But we all knew he had been badly wounded and was in poor shape.

We took over the campsite, finishing off the preparation of the food the Zealots had been preparing. Then we stripped their bodies of their clothes, money, arms and valuables.

"Is there anything my size," said Affa, smiling with his chubby hands patting his belly.

"Here, see if you can squeeze into these," said Luce, throwing him the largest shirt and breeches.

"That was a bit of luck. We were in need of a change of clothes. With these clothes and the beards we have now grown, nobody will take a second look at us. Maybe we can travel a bit more by day now," said Affa.

"Yeah, and look what I've found," said TJ, pulling behind him a mule and a horse. Affa smiled again.

"Now we're getting somewhere," he said.

The next few days were difficult, though. We were worried about Dess who was suffering badly from his injuries. We now realised that he had suffered more than the single knife wound to his stomach, and we had had to strip the bandages and have a closer look in the daylight. Affa, who seemed to know what to do to make him comfortable, had patched him up as well as possible with the rudimentary materials we had at our disposal. TJ, who was probably closer to Dess than any of us, stayed by him as we carried on our trek; much more slowly now because of Dess's injuries. We had tried to seat Dess on the mule but he was too unsteady and kept starting to fall sideways off the animal. Then we tried seating him on the horse, with TJ sitting behind him to hold him from falling. This seemed to work reasonably well, but we still had to walk the horse slowly as every jolt was painful to Dess. With Dess on the horse, we were able to make a little more progress. And by evening, when we stopped to make overnight camp, Dess seemed to be a little better and certainly in higher spirits.

We were still in the habit of posting a lookout whenever we stopped, and when I got up early to relieve Affa, he told me he had a job to do before he rested, and that he needed the horse. He quietly set off back down the way we had already travelled.

We were having some breakfast when he returned, smiling broadly, and carrying four or five stout poles he had cut and trimmed from the roadside a few miles back.

"Now then you, lot," he said, "Watch and learn. We're going to make a Drag!"

"A Drag?" someone asked, "What's a Drag?"

"Watch and learn," Affa replied.

After a quick bite to eat, he got to work. He cut some poles shorter and fashioned a stretcher which had short carry handles at one end and very long ones at the other. Then, backing the horse between the long carry handles, he secured them to the horse and walked it forward a few paces to ensure the stretcher dragged effectively on the ground without pulling away from the horse. The stretcher crosspieces, he covered with some of the covers and blankets we had, to make it more comfortable.

"There you are," said Affa, "a nice comfortable Drag for Dess to lie on!"

After Affa had a brief rest and some more food, we struck camp. TJ and I helped Dess onto his new mode of transport, tying him on so that he was comfortable and secure before we set off once again.

Although Dess's condition had slowed our progress down, by pulling him along on the Drag we were able to move a little quicker now. And Dess seemed much more comfortable. I led the horse and TJ walked beside Dess to keep an eye on him.

At the next rest stop, Dess seemed to be a little better and even a little chatty. But as the day wore on, TJ asked me to slow the pace down a little as Dess seemed to be slipping in and out of consciousness. Soon, we were travelling very slowly, and when we came to a suitable place to stop, Affa decided that we should set up camp to give Dess a chance to relax properly. Just before we stopped, Dess seemed to perk up a little, and even said he thought he could eat something. We were pleased at this, as he had eaten very little since he had sustained his injury, and we felt that he needed to build up his strength. We were unpacking our gear when TJ started to unfasten Dess's securing straps to release him from the Drag. Suddenly he shouted.

"Boss," he said, "I can't bring him round!" Affa grabbed the medical kit and ran over to Dess. Crouching beside him, he wiped the soldier's face, spoke quietly to him, and felt for a pulse. After a few minutes of trying to revive him, however, he stood up slowly and sighed. "He's gone lads… we've lost him," he said sadly.

"What…he was just chatting about having something to eat five minutes ago!" said TJ, wide eyed.

"Aye, lad," said Affa sadly, "but he's gone now." He shook his head. "It sometimes happens that way. A good lad was Dess, a good lad," He turned and walked away, as the rest of us looked at each other and then at Dess, hardly able to comprehend what had happened. TJ started to speak to Dess, to shake him and to slap his face but to no avail; he was dead.

"I've never known anything like that before," said TJ, "It's unbelievable, just unbelievable…"

Affa was silently and sullenly unbuckling gear from the mule. After a few minutes, he came back to us.

"Right, lads," he said in a gruff and business-like manner. "Let's give the lad a good send-off; we'll bury him over there. Make a good job of it, lads. He deserves the best we can do for him."

Chapter 11

Things were different after we lost Dess. After he became injured, we had been unable to travel overland because every jolt had been painful to him. We had had to go slowly on well-worn pathways and keep a keen lookout, and we had only just avoided coming into contact with other travellers on a number of occasions. Now, we decided to travel east once more, away from the possibility of encountering anyone else—across even more rugged and harsh terrain than before. We turned the horse and mule loose, knowing that not only would it be difficult to feed them, but also that the terrain would be difficult for them to negotiate and that they would only slow us down.

The loss of Dess took its toll in other ways too. Up to then, we had all been fairly positive. And even though we had lost Porky, we all realised any one of us could have suffered a snake bite at any time in this awful country. We had been sure in what we were doing; confident that this was the only thing we could do and that the only alternative would be death, and a very cruel death at that. We had even discussed the things we were going to do when we achieved our freedom—the happy times we were going to enjoy. After Dess's death though, we all seemed to lose interest in anything other than travelling on to the North-Western coast as quickly as possible and getting away to safety. We trudged on in sullen silence, each man absorbed in his own thoughts and fears, unwilling to share them with each other.

TJ took it worse than the rest of us. Dess had been a good mate to him; they had joined up within a few weeks of each other, trained together, and managed to get posted to the same unit. They had shared each other's successes and each other's failures, always been there for each other. Now at rest stops, TJ would sit quietly, gazing into the fire or staring absently into the far distance. Affa tried to bring him out of it, with compassion at first, then quite brusquely by telling him to pull himself together, reminding him that we had all lost good mates in the past, but a soldier just has to dust himself off and then get on with it. "Life has to go on," he said.

But it didn't seem to help much. TJ remained silent and sullen. The loss of Dess had taken a drastic toll on him. It had affected me, too.

Luce, TJ and I were chatting one evening while Affa was on watch.

"I'm just not convinced that we did the right thing now, Luce," I said, "I wonder sometimes if we would have been better staying, like Cass did, and taking our chances telling the truth."

"What is the truth then?" said Luce, making sparks fly upwards as he poked the fire, "That the dead body we were guarding just vanished before our eyes? Or somebody just pinched it from under our noses? Or maybe, he came to back to life, pushed away the stone single-handedly, and without making any noise, tiptoed past us into the night? Which one do you believe?"

"Well, I don't know. But we have come all this way, wandering in the wilderness, looking over our shoulders all the time, living on our nerves, jumping at every unusual noise. We've lost two blokes and achieved very little. Cass probably had the right idea."

"Cass was dead before we left the cemetery, and you know it!" said Luce, throwing more kindling on the fire.

"Dead?" both TJ and I said together, "What do you mean?"

Luce looked at us with an expression of amazed amusement. "Don't look so innocent! I don't believe you haven't guessed!" he said.

"What are you on about," said TJ, beginning now to lose his temper.

"Do you think Affa took him away for a quiet chat when they went up behind the far cemetery wall?"

"Well…yes," I said, a little lamely.

"Yeah, me too," added TJ more forcefully, "Why shouldn't we think that?"

Luce shook his head and laughed, "I can't believe that you're both so naive. Do you honestly think Affa would have risked all our lives by leaving Cass alive?"

"What!!!" said TJ, jumping to his feet, "I can hardly believe what you are saying! Affa just murdered him in cold blood?"

"Murdered is a strong word," said Luce, shaking his head.

"What word would you use then?" TJ was really fired up now. He paced back and forth, running his fingers through his hair. "No, no, this is all wrong, all wrong," he said, turning away.

"Listen," said Luce, "If Affa had let him live, we'd ALL have ended up nailed to crosses like the three blokes we just executed. Would you have wanted that? I certainly wouldn't. Isn't it better that one man dies instead of all of us? At least Cass didn't suffer like we all would have done—including him—by being crucified."

I was stunned too. I had never imagined that Cass was walking to his death as he walked away from us with Affa's arm around his shoulder. But I could understand what Luce meant, and having witnessed my first crucifixion with all its pain and suffering, I was glad that I had been spared that ordeal. But TJ was incensed. Taking an aggressive stance, he pointed a finger at Luce.

"Now you listen, Luce. You had better keep him away from me, or else *he* could end up with his throat cut."

Still seated by the fire, Luce held up his hand, "You try anything like that, TJ, and you'll have me to deal with. We owe Affa plenty. We would all be dead now if it hadn't been for him. He's got us this far and he'll get us away. Now pull yourself together, and let's put all this behind us. We need each other now even more than ever, and we all need Affa especially! I certainly can't find my way through this desolate, awful place, can you?"

TJ's eyes were filled with loathing for both Affa and Luce now. For a long moment, he stood facing Luce off before turning and stomping away. As he did so, Affa appeared.

"What's going on? What's all the shouting about? Do you want to get us all killed?"

"It's ok, Boss," said Luce calmly, "Just a misunderstanding. Everything's ok." Affa looked at Luce and then at TJ's back as he walked away from the camp area. He turned without speaking and went back to his picket position.

The tension from then on was palpable. TJ now trusted no-one. He would walk at the back of the column so that he could keep his eye on the rest of us, and refused to go any further forward. He was sullen, quiet, hardly spoke to anyone, and refused to speak to Affa at all. He would do what was expected of him and no more. Affa tried a few times to speak to him, to find out what the problem was, but each time, TJ would simply walk away. Finally, Affa challenged him as he was walking away from one of these stand-offs.

"Justus, don't you turn your back on me. I'm sick and tired of this stupidity! Come back here!"

"Or what?" said TJ, turning to face Affa, his eyes once more filled with anger and loathing, "Will you stab me in the back like you did Cass?"

"Oh, that's what it is!" said Affa, his expression reflecting the fact that he had just realised the reason for TJ's resentment.

"Don't be such an idiot! Do you think I wanted to kill him? It was either him or us—all of us."

"Don't give me that; you're a liar and a backstabber. You probably murdered Dess too! Don't turn your back on me mate, or you'll be sorry!"

Affa took a step forward and held TJ threateningly by the front of his shirt.

"I'm not your mate, I'm your Boss—I'm still your Boss and don't you forget it. And don't threaten me again or it's you who will be sorry." He let TJ go. "I did my best for Dess. He would have died within a couple of hours of being hit if it hadn't been for me." Poking a forefinger he went on, "I got you this far. You'd already be a dead man if it wasn't for me. Now pull yourself together and let's try to get to the coast. Once we get away from this lousy country, you can go your own way and I'll go mine, but until then, we all need each other." Softening his tone, he turned to the rest of us. "Now come on, lads, let's have some food and get some rest. We've all had enough of this. The sooner we get to the Northern coast, the better now."

TJ seemed a little less hostile in the days following his confrontation with Affa. He was still withdrawn, quiet and very pensive—but not aggressive in the way he had been before. Luce and I could tell that Affa was making an effort to be conciliatory with him, and I think TJ felt it too. But still, he often seemed distant; he would still stare vacantly at the ground in front of himself or into the far distance as if deep in thought. He was having difficulty in sleeping, and would walk around listlessly at night as the rest of us tried to rest and renew our strength. We found it difficult to relax because we no longer trusted him and felt that he was irrational enough to attack any or all of us without warning at any time.

Time now seemed to drag by. I was amazed how Affa had so confidently and competently led us through the desolate, harsh, unfamiliar landscape which to me all looked the same in every direction. But using the stars at night and the position of the sun during the day, he had led us South, then West, then North, and now we were travelling in a North-Westerly direction towards the Northern coast, many miles from Jerusalem.

At last, we noticed the comforting sight and sound of seabirds flying high above us, indicating that we were approaching the coast. But even this didn't hearten TJ in the way it did the rest of us.

At a rest stop, Affa tried to jolly TJ along a little.

"Not long now, lad—nearly home," he said with a smile. "Are you a bit happier now?" he asked TJ.

TJ looked at him for a moment, then sighed heavily. "Not really. I don't know how I feel. Yes I do—I feel empty. I feel that we lost Dess for no good reason, and I still don't understand why you had to murder Cass."

Affa stood up threateningly, but Luce intervened. "Calm down, chaps," he said, "this is getting us nowhere. Just put up with each other for a few more days and then we will be free."

Even at this stage, Affa still insisted that we post a lookout when we were resting and at night, and to be fair, TJ still did his share of the picket duty. But once more his attitude was deteriorating and we were becoming concerned about him again.

A couple of days later, I came off lookout duty in the middle of the night and handed over to TJ while the others were still asleep. TJ was wide awake and sitting up, his back against a rock, apparently lost in his thoughts. He didn't speak to me when I handed over to him but simply stood up, kicked away the horse blanket which had been covering him, and made his way silently to the lookout point. I was tired and it wasn't long before I was fast asleep. I was woken some time later, however, just as dawn was breaking, by a shout from Luce. I looked around and drew my dagger, thinking we were being attacked by Zealots or, even worse, by Roman soldiers. Then I saw Affa running towards the direction of the shouting. Quickly I got up, grabbed my sword and weapon belt, and ran after him. I soon caught up with him. And as we rounded a bend, we almost bumped into Luce. He was standing facing towards us, catching his breath, leaning forward with his hands on his knees.

"What's up?" shouted Affa. Luce jerked his thumb over his shoulder, shaking his head as he did so.

"Tried getting him down but couldn't manage it," he said breathlessly. We both looked where he had pointed. There, near to a grove of rushes and a small water spring was a solitary tree. It was a big strong tree with heavy boughs. Hanging by the neck from the strongest bough was TJ. He was dead.

Chapter 12

We only stopped long enough to bury TJ. None of us could face a meal, and so we packed our gear and started off once more. Now we were more determined than ever to get our heads down and move as quickly as we could. Weary of continually being on the move, looking over our shoulders, and with the anxiety of the possibility of running into Roman soldiers, Zealots or even suspicious locals, we just wanted now to get to the coast and get away.

By now, we were travelling through the more populated coastal plain and aiming for the coast north of Antioch. Affa knew that there were a number of small fishing villages up there, and felt certain that we would be able to hitch a ride from a fishing boat to get us away from the mainland. The nearer we got to the coast, the more revitalised and re-invigorated the three of us became. We could smell the coast; we felt we could even taste freedom!

We were travelling regularly by day now and felt somewhat more relaxed—so much so that when we came upon a small township, we decided to risk looking out for an inn where we could enjoy a decent meal and drink for a change. We all had long hair and beards now, and with the clothes we had taken from the Zealots, we knew no one would give us a second glance. As we entered the settlement though, we noticed smoke rising from one of the houses and heard a lot of shouting and panicky commotion going on. Cautiously, we made our way to the scene of the fire and found a large house which had outbuildings and corralled yards with goats, sheep and a well. Smoke, flames and sparks were pouring out of the roof and a couple of men were shouting and frantically trying to prise open a door while women were screaming, waving their arms and weeping. Instinctively, the three of us ran towards the burning house. When the men saw us, they frantically indicated to us that they needed help because there was someone inside.

The fire was burning fiercely throughout the house and as I had outrun Affa and Luce, I started to help the men prise open the door. It was wedged closed by burning joists which had fallen from the roof and was almost impossible to shift. However, adrenalin kicked in and together we managed to make enough room to get inside. I pushed the older man out of the way, and pulled my coat across my face and head for protection from the heat and smoke, allowing just enough gap for me to see out as I started to squeeze through the gap we had made in the doorway. The smoke was dense, but I had already seen two young people inside. There was a boy of about 12 years and a little girl about five or six—both trapped at the far side of a room which was strewn with burning debris and filling up with smoke. I screwed up my eyes against the acrid smoke and managed to get inside. I realised now that the house was different to other Judean houses I had ever come across in that it had a wooden floor over a basement stable beneath. I started to move gingerly across the room, and made my way towards the kids. They had seen me and were crying, waving and shouting for help through the noise of the burning joists and woodwork. The older man had started to follow me into the room. But the heat and the smoke had been too much for him, and he had gone back outside, and was now on his knees, coughing and choking with the effects of the smoke. The heat was intense, and as I tried to get across the floor to the kids, crouching as I did so to avoid being choked by the dense smoke, I could hear and feel the floorboards and joists giving slightly beneath me with every step I took. At last, I managed to get near enough to reach the children, and the boy pushed the girl in front of him, and she reached out her tiny hands. I grasped her by the wrists and pulled but she still seemed to be trapped, and I couldn't get her out and was afraid of hurting her if I pulled too hard. In desperation, her brother gave her a hard push and I finally had her. I clutched her tightly under my arm and covered her with the folds of my cloak to protect her from the heat and smoke. The boy, however, had fallen backwards with the effort of pushing his sister, and I realised I would have to take her out and come back for him. I shouted and indicated to him that I would come back, then I carefully picked my way back out of the room, avoiding the burning debris, conscious all the time that my next step might see me falling through the floor and into the basement below. By the time I had got to the doorway, Affa and Luce were there, both still struggling to get the door open again as it had fallen back closed after I had gone inside. I continued to struggle towards the doorway and then heard a shout from the window beside the door; it had been blocked by burning woodwork until now but Affa had managed to move enough of it to be able to reach inside and take the girl from me. I shouted to him that there was another child inside and that I was going back to try to get him out. Affa shouted back that it was too dangerous; that the roof was about to collapse any minute. But I was convinced that I could save the lad, and I had no hesitation in turning back into the heat and smoke inside the house. The smoke was choking me, my eyes were watering, my clothes were so hot that they were smoking. And I was sure they would burst into flames at any minute, but I could not countenance leaving the boy to be burned alive inside the building. As I turned to go back for the lad, my breath was taken away as Luce threw a full bucket of water over me to saturate and cool my clothes. I waved my thanks to him, and carefully, I made my way back towards the lad. Again, as I took each step, I could feel the wooden floor moving beneath my feet; it was even more unstable than it had been before, and continually, there were big pieces of burning woodwork falling from above—some missing me by only inches. The lad had by now almost squeezed himself through the small gap he had pushed the girl through, but now there was other burning debris between us. I managed with some difficulty to reach him, however, and grabbed him by the wrists as I had done with his sister, and pulled him towards me. His face was blackened by the smoke and he had white marks down his cheeks from the tears which had run from his eyes. His clothes were smouldering, and it looked and smelled as if some of his hair had been on fire. He clung tightly to me, and I turned to try to make my way towards the doorway where I could see Luce holding open the damaged and burning door so that I could get out. He was beckoning, telling me to hurry, shouting that the roof was about to fall in. I was almost halfway across the room with the lad clutched tightly in my arms when I heard an ominous rumble followed by an almighty crashing noise above me. I felt intense heat, saw falling joists, debris and sparks, and then…blackness.

*****

I don't know for how long I was unconscious. When I finally came round, I was lying on the ground twenty or thirty metres from the house which was still burning and had a thick pall of smoke over it which reached high into the cloudless blue sky. Affa was kneeling over me with a wet cloth in his hands. When he saw me open my eyes, he gently stroked my face with the cloth. It was cool and very welcome, and Affa's voice sounded reassuring and calming. I tried to sit up.

"Ok, lad, you're all right now, just relax, lie still for a while longer, you're gonna be ok now…"

"What happened…is the kid ok?" I asked, feeling weak and somewhat disoriented and bewildered.

"Yeah, the kid's fine—part of the roof came down on you, it was a bit of a mess, but you're ok now."

I lay back down, utterly exhausted but glad that between us, we had been able to rescue the youngsters. I could still hear the crackle of the burning house, but other than that, there seemed to be a strange and eerie silence, despite the large group of onlookers which had formed in front of it. I felt there was something wrong. Affa was still cooling my face with the cloth he had soaked in water.

"Everybody ok then?" I asked lamely.

"Aye, lad," said Affa, "…well…everybody except Luce anyway."

"Luce? Why, what's up with him?"

Affa sighed heavily.

"We lost Luce," he said simply.

"Lost him?" I shouted, struggling up on to my elbows and looking round to see where Luce was.

"Easy lad, easy," said Affa, "When part of the roof fell in on you, Luce went in for you both. The kid was still conscious and Luce managed to get him back to the doorway. Then he just turned straight around to go back for you. He managed to drag you to the doorway and push you near enough for me to get you through the door when the rest of the roof collapsed on top of him and the floor gave way. He never stood a chance."

"Oh no, no, no, that was my fault, it should have been me—not him!"

"No, lad, it was nobody's fault. We would have all done the same for each other. Just one of them things that happen," he said sadly. He got to his feet, wiped his face with the damp cloth he still had in his hands, and started to walk wearily away.

"He was a good lad was Luce, a good lad," he said, seemingly to himself. He turned briefly to me.

"Just me and you now, lad—just me and you."

Chapter 13

Even though we both felt the despondency and sadness of having lost so many of our friends and colleagues, Affa and I were heartened by the fact that we were very close to the coast now and indeed, to that part of the coast which we were fairly sure would be safe. We buried Luce, had a meal, and rested briefly in an effort to regain our strength, then once more we were on our trek to the coast. The landscape was now becoming much more green and luxuriant; there were lots of seabirds above us, and we could even hear the sea. We became much more relaxed, more companions now than NCO and soldier, although Affa still gave the orders and made the decisions—but that was fine by me. I knew I owed Affa a debt of gratitude for effectively saving my life, and I was happy to put my trust in him to get me all the way to freedom.

We came in sight of a small fishing village in the late afternoon. Affa decided that we shouldn't enter it until we had made a proper recce and were sure in our own minds that there was no Roman garrison posted there or nearby, and that the people in the village were not going to be hostile to us. We pitched camp a good way away from the village in a very quiet and secluded area and had some food before discussing what to do next. We decided to get a good night's rest, even though

Affa still insisted that we sleep in shifts and take it in turns to keep watch in the way we had all through our flight from Jerusalem. And then early next morning, Affa would go on his own into the village and see what he could find out about the people there. I was to stay at the campsite, well hidden, until Affa returned and reported. Then we would decide what action to take.

In the morning, Affa seemed a little apprehensive, so much so that I suggested maybe I should go instead of him. "No, lad," he said in his usual manner, "leave this to me. I know the lingo. I've got the experience and I know all the angles. I'll be back soon." He wagged his finger at me in the way he always did when he was making an important point. "Don't you move from here or show yourself under any circumstances until I get back. Understand?"

I watched him disappear down the track leading to the village, then I settled back into our camouflaged campsite. I was tempted to relax and get some more sleep, but I was also anxious that once the village woke up, people might come past our hiding place and I wanted to be fully alert. In any case, I knew that anxiety would prevent me from getting any significant rest.

The morning dragged on. No one came anywhere near our campsite—I wasn't even troubled by any foraging animal. As time wore on, I began to become restless, getting up and looking down the track for any sign of Affa on his way back. I ate only cold food, mainly jerky, not wanting to make a fire. And by early afternoon, I was fairly certain that Affa had run into trouble. I decided that if he hadn't arrived back by nightfall, I would use the cover of darkness to go into the village and search for him.

It was later in the afternoon when I heard a noise nearby and, looking out I saw Affa coming back up the track alone. I was so relieved at seeing him that I broke cover and went out to meet him.

"What do you think you're doing!" he snapped when he saw me.

"Where have you been? Is everything ok?"

"If it wasn't, there would be no hope for us now, would there? Where's your weapon? For all you know, there could be a gang of them behind me, using me as a hostage or bait! Haven't you learnt anything from me?"

"Sorry, Boss," I said, crestfallen. As usual, Affa was right. If there had been a problem, I would have played right into their hands.

"Listen," he went on, "We're in luck for once. It seems ok. Nobody wants to ask a lot of questions, they are all quite amicable—the ones I've seen anyway. I've got us a billet and the people are ok."

"Do they know about me?"

"Yeah, that's not a problem."

So, what's the story—about us I mean; what's our cover story?"

"Just weary travellers, on the run from the Romans for being members of the resistance would you believe!"

"Knowing you, I would believe it!" I said with a grin.

"By the way, your name is Joseph and mine is John. Come on, lad, our digs will be ready. We will still take turns to keep our eyes open during the night—you never can be too careful. But I'm fairly sure they are ok here. Oh—and by the way, you can't hear very well and are a mute—save you getting us into trouble by speaking Italian or saying something in Hebrew which even you don't understand!"

The house was quite big and commanded a good view of the rest of the small village. The village had never been garrisoned by Roman soldiers although a unit had briefly stayed there once—a long time ago when they were chasing resistance fighters. It was a quiet, sleepy village, very much out of the way, very insignificant—exactly what we were looking for in fact. The only problem was that the only boat which would have been big enough and strong enough to take us any distance away from the mainland was currently under repair and had been for some time. From his discussions with the people he had spoken to, Affa was sure though that once the boat was repaired and re-commissioned, its owners would be prepared to take us.

The family who were lodging us were very personable and understanding. We became fairly certain that they had guessed that our story was only a cover, but we were prepared to work hard for our keep and they recognised that. Affa had offered to pay for our board and lodging with Roman cash we told them we had stolen, but it was only of use to them if they went to a big town or city with a Roman Garrison there. So, our hard work was much more valuable to them. We started to relax. Within a few days, we were starting to enjoy life once again.

Affa seemed to take to the family who were billeting us. He got on really well with the father of the family; and also the man's wife appreciated the fact that we were willing to help in the home as well as out in the fields with her husband and sons. The kids treated Affa like a long-lost favourite Uncle, and even though the boat repair seemed to be taking an awful long time, Affa didn't seem to be too worried. Soon, I was no longer a mute or hard of hearing, and the family were helping me to improve on my Hebrew.

I have to admit that the lifestyle was very appealing to me too, but at the same time, the fact that we were deserters from the Roman Army nagged at the back of my mind, and I was still eager to get away from the mainland and into an area where there was less chance that the Roman Authorities would ever catch up with me. Affa was sure by now that the heat would be off us.

"They haven't caught us," he said, "and the Jews have paid some guys and conned them into saying that they were the ones on duty at the cemetery and that someone stole the body. I wouldn't like to think what might have happened to them, but rather them than us! So Pilate won't want us to re-appear again, he will want us to simply disappear—for all anyone else knows, the squad who lost the body has paid the price for it and that's that." I certainly hoped he was right. Agatopus, the senior military police officer in Judea, was a vindictive man who resented any attempt to humiliate or outwit him. And I wouldn't have been surprised if we were still on his hit list. In addition, I had heard stories about some sort of Roman secret military police who didn't ever forget about anyone or anything, and I was still a little uneasy. I wouldn't be happy until I was well away from the mainland and the direct influence of the Roman Empire.

We stayed with our new friends for several months, because the repair of the boat seemed to have stalled for some reason. At last though, we got word that the boat was once again seaworthy and that we were to be taken off the mainland. We had been given less than a week's notice because the boat had been sold and would shortly be leaving the village for good. However, we soon had our gear all packed and were ready to make our final break for freedom. But as soon as we were told about our sailing date, I noticed that Affa began to become unsettled. When we were alone, I tackled him about it.

"Are you looking forward to getting away then? Our adventure is nearly over!" I said to him with a smile.

He was quiet and pensive for a long moment.

"Yeah, I suppose I am…" he said at last, "I was beginning to think we would never make it. But here we are, all kitted up and ready to go," he continued. He got up and walked outside. It was then I realised that he was happy and settled with this family. I began to wonder if I would be making the trip alone.

On the afternoon of our departure, the whole of our adopted family and even some neighbours and friends came down to the shore, laden with our gear and with gifts which the kids had made and given to us. Our host's wife and kids were upset—some of them crying, and even her husband was obviously moved at the fact that we were leaving. We loaded our gear, made our fond farewells, climbed into the boat, and settled down for the voyage. But just before we cast off, Affa stood up and spoke to the skipper. I didn't know what they were saying but then Affa started to become agitated and started with his finger wagging.

"Hey," I shouted, "what's the problem?"

"No problem," said Affa, starting to collect up his gear. "No problem, lad—I'm going to have to leave you, that's all."

"Leave me?"

"Aye, lad." He was already stepping out of the boat. He turned to me.

"Tertius, lad—this is the only place I've ever felt at home, ever felt actually wanted. I'm not gonna find anywhere else where I can be as settled as I have been over the last few months. I'm sorry, lad, I'm really sorry. You'll be all right, you're away now. Make a good new life for yourself and don't ever look back. Oh, and I've agreed with the skipper here to pay him for taking both of us even though he's only taking you, so don't let him take any more money from you." He reached back into the boat and held out a strong chubby hand, "Look after yourself, Tertius, and don't ever forget the things I've taught you. We've come through a lot together, and I'll never forget you."

He waded back out of the water and the man and his whole family came running towards him, smiling and laughing, taking all his gear from him and hugging him. The smallest of the children jumped up, and soon, her arm was around his neck and Affa was carrying her in his left arm while he held her brother's hand with his right hand. They were all so absorbed with each other that they didn't even notice that the boat had cast off. We were about fifty metres from shore when Affa eventually turned and looked towards me. I waved, he let go of the lad's hand and waved back. He hesitated for a moment watching the boat, then turned, and took hold of the lad's hand once more before continuing to walk up the beach. The timbers creaked and the sail flapped, distracting me. When I looked back to the beach, it was deserted. I was beginning my new life—alone.

Epilogue

Had I written this memoire a year ago, there would be little else to tell. I got away scot free, crossed the seas, and made a new life in civvy street. I was never ever challenged by anyone as having been a deserter from the Roman Army, and eventually I settled down, learned the local language, married a lovely local girl and raised a family I have always been proud of. When, some years ago now, Christian missionaries came to the area where I live, I became a convert. It was only then when I realised that Jesus Christ was the 'king' I had helped crucify all those years before at Golgotha. At first, I found it difficult to come to terms with, but with the help of the missionaries and my wife (who had been converted before me, and in fact, had helped to lead me to the Christian faith), I came to terms with it and realised that because of my conversion and my faith, God had forgiven me. I became a lay preacher within the Christian church, helping to grow not just my local Church but occasionally travelling further away to help spread the word. Then, just a few months ago, I received a call from a colleague Pastor. He asked me if I would be willing to travel with him on a three-month missionary journey which he was arranging and organising. I consulted with my wife and we decided I should go. And that's when I found out that the journey would, just by chance, include a visit to the coastal town from where I had escaped many years earlier. My wife knew all about my past, but had no worries about me going back. And although even after so many years I was still a little uneasy about it, she convinced me to go by saying simply, "You should go…"

It was a thrilling missionary journey, very successful, with many converts. We had been travelling and preaching at various centres for almost three months before we eventually arrived at the shores which I had left all those years ago. Much had changed; the small sleepy village had grown into a busy bustling township, and although I made some tenuous enquiries about Affa and the family I had briefly stayed with those years before, I was unable to find anyone who knew them.

As we chatted to the local Christian pastor, we were told that now there was a Roman garrison in the town. I have to admit that this information took me by surprise, and I was a little apprehensive about being seen and recognised by Roman soldiers. The reason for the garrison having been set up there was that the Roman occupation forces had established that the township had become a meeting point for an active and really quite vicious Zealot resistance movement working against the Roman Authorities. These Zealots had found a cruel and callous way to 'kill two birds with one stone' as it were. They despised the occupation forces, and had an almost equal hatred for Christians; their plan was to carry out armed resistance against the Roman occupation troops, and then lay the blame on Jewish Christian converts; planting contrived evidence on them; then informing on them; and leading the Romans to them. That way they caused harm to Rome, and at the same time, caused harm to the fledgling Christian church.

We prayed together, and tried to think of practical ways we could help. Then we learned that there was to be a crucifixion at the Roman execution site of some local Christians who had been falsely accused of crimes against the occupying forces. The local pastor asked if we would go to the crucifixion in order to give support to the Christians who were to be executed in this cruel and inhuman manner.

By chance, the execution site turned out to be at almost the same spot as Affa and I had camped when we first came to the town after our flight from Jerusalem. I shuddered at the thought of seeing another crucifixion; I knew it would bring back the bitter memories of not only the crucifixion of Jesus Christ, but also it would remind me of all the colleagues I had lost and of the times which I had long ago tried to put behind me. However, I recognised the need and counted it a privilege to help and support my brother Christians at this dark and difficult time in their lives. The possibility of anyone recognising me was, of course, a concern, but the words of my wife when she said, "You should go," I felt applied to this situation too, and I agreed to go.

It was late in the afternoon of the day of the execution, when we arrived at the execution site. And the sight in the distance of five crosses and the cries and moans of the prisoners who were by then already on the crosses took me suddenly and sickeningly back over the years to the time when I had helped to crucify Jesus Christ. The thought chilled my body and my soul. I prayed a silent prayer for help to carry out my difficult and grim task.

The execution site was set out much the same as Golgotha had been; it was about the same size and had that same aura of hopelessness and smell of death. I recognised much of the equipment lying around—the hammers, leather nail pouches, the Legbreaker, wineskins containing pain-deadening potions, even the 'Longjohn' spear for establishing death. My stomach churned at the sight and my thoughts were in turmoil, but I knew that for the sake of the poor souls who were suffering for their Christian faith—a faith which I myself now embraced—I had to put my own feelings to one side and try to give what support I could.

Although we were unable to tell the prisoners that we were fellow Christians, there to intercede for them and not merely to watch them die, we did know that they had been told that we would be there. And I was sure that because of our demeanour, they would know who we were, and would find comfort and strength from our presence there. And I was certain that our silent prayers would also help them to get through the almost unbearable agony of crucifixion.

We walked along the line of crosses, stopping in front of each one, praying silently in our hearts for the soul of each of our suffering brothers. Most of the men were close to death, but most managed to briefly look at us. Their eyes showed recognition of who we were and why we were there. I like to think that their eyes softened a little and their pain eased somewhat because of our support, and especially because of our prayers.

We came at last to the fifth cross. The man was much older than the other prisoners, and was obviously in great pain. His eyes were tightly closed and his lips pursed as if struggling to cope with his great agonising pain. We stood before him and I closed my eyes, earnestly praying for the man, asking that God would take him quickly and ease his pain. After I had prayed, I looked up at the man, hoping to give him some comfort from the expression of compassion and love on my face.

The man looked down at me, his face still contorted in agony. He struggled to push down with his feet, trying to ease the pressure on his chest and lungs so that he could breathe—and then the strangest thing happened. The man, who obviously had only minutes rather than hours left to live, who was suffering the most cruel torture, who could hardly breathe, who was naked and held to the wooden scaffold by nails through his hands and feet, and who was covered in sweat and blood, suddenly looked back at me, staring intently through eyes that were dark and full of grief and agony. As I looked into the man's eyes I seemed to see a different person. Something stirred in the back of my mind—some vague recognition…did I know this man from somewhere? As we continued to look into each other's eyes, I could hardly believe the fact that he actually tried to smile. A weak, faint and weary smile, but a smile all the same; and not just a smile, a smile of recognition. He seemed to know me. I was just about to turn to my colleague to ask who this man was when the man's lips began to move. Hoarsely and with obvious difficulty, he started to say something. Unbelievably, it seemed like he was speaking Italian. I listened and watched intently as I tried to make out what he was trying to say to me.

"God…bless…you…" There was another word too but I couldn't make out what it was at first. Then it suddenly came to me… "God bless you, LAD!" In a second, the realisation flooded over and through me. How could I have missed it! Of course, it was Affa.

Affa's head dropped wearily to his chest, the effort of trying to speak had exhausted him. I turned to my colleague, my mind racing, my heart in my mouth.

"Why are they crucifying a Roman Army deserter along with these Christians?" I asked, totally confused and not a little worried that I may have inadvertently walked into a trap.

"Roman Army deserter?" he replied, as confused now as I was. "No, no, this is John. He has lived in the town for many years, everybody knows John. A great chap—would do anything for anyone. He is a local farmer—a real pillar of the Christian church here, a local lay preacher. I don't know anyone who speaks ill of him. It's so sad, he will be greatly missed." With a confused expression on his face, he continued, "What made you think he was a Roman Army deserter?"

"Sorry, sorry, it's me. I was mistaking him for someone else…sorry." I looked back at Affa. His face looked calmer now; the pain had left his eyes. He looked briefly towards Heaven, then closed his eyes. His head once more fell onto his chest. His torment was over.

Affa was dead.

*****

Post Script

When I first met him, I didn't like Affa much. I felt he was self-opinionated, bombastic, and, worst of all, self-serving. He knew how to work the system, and if he hurt, upset or trod on anyone in the process of getting what he wanted, it didn't matter at all to him. Then as I started to serve under him, I realised that in spite of all these unfortunate characteristics, he was a good soldier, a man who did his best to look after the men in his care, and to teach them how to look after themselves and each other as well. Admittedly, he looked after himself too, sometimes at the expense of others, but never of us. And the thing I came to appreciate most of all was that he allowed all of us to benefit from the fact that he knew all the angles and exploited them. And without doubt it is a fact that without him I would have been dead many years ago. And I may well have died a cruel and tortuous death too, nailed to a cross.

Over the years following my Christian conversion, stories filtered back to us from Missionaries regarding the circumstances surrounding Christ's crucifixion. The information Affa had got from his colleague turned out to be pretty much dead on – the story came back to us that the soldiers guarding the tomb had been Temple Guards, not

Roman Soldiers at all, and they had said that someone had overpowered them and stolen the body. After their 'confessions' they hadn't been heard of again. Barabbas was in fact freed by Pilate – but was found dead in mysterious circumstances two days later outside the city walls.

Much has been made by Jesus Christ's followers of the crown of thorns Affa wove and pressed onto Jesus's head before the crucifixion. A simple, seemingly insignificant act, carried out by a man who at the time was cruel hearted and who simply wanted to make a joke at the expense of the prisoner in his charge. And yet this has been taken by Jesus' followers and used down the intervening years as a significant and recognisable symbol of martyrdom—Christ's martyrdom—A cruel gesture by a cruel man which was completely turned on its head.

I just wish that there was a way I could let the whole world know that even cruel heartless men such as we were then, may be redeemed by the blood of the man we so willingly crucified...

The End